FECAL TERROR

David Bernstein

David Bernstein

Bizarro Pulp Press
www.BIZARROPULPPRESS.com
David Bernstein Copyright © 2013 Fecal Terror

ISBN-13: 978-0615867137
ISBN-10: 0615867138

Printed in the USA.

CHAPTER 1

With his right hand, Barry held the bunny by its ears. In his left was a large kitchen knife, the blade pressed against the critter's neck. The rabbit squealed and kicked its hind legs wildly, understanding on some level that its life was in peril.

Cringing as he did so, Barry drew the blade across the bunny's throat. Blood spewed from the slit, coating his knife-wielding hand, part of his chest and chin in red. The fluffy critter kicked harder for a few moments, but as more blood left its body its struggles slowed until it moved no more.

Barry stared at the bunny as it swayed like a hanged man, its white fur now matted and slick with glossy redness. The forest surrounding him was still.

He moved the rabbit over the sacrificial goblet he had ordered from a satanic online store, and watched the blood drain. When he was finished, the bunny no longer dripping as much, he held the beast's corpse out and said, "I offer this sacrifice to Benzonah the Insidious, demon of all demons." Barry placed the dead rabbit on a tan ceramic dinner dish he had taken from his house, knowing his mother would raise holy hell if she knew what he was using it for.

Next, Barry opened a small Ziplock bag containing goldfish eyes, and dumped them into the goblet of rabbit blood. He was supposed to use a human eye, but discovered finding them to be difficult, and he wasn't about to kidnap someone and scoop out an eye, let alone kill for it. So, earlier that week, he'd purchased three Feeder-fish, and plucked out their eyeballs before flushing the blind freshwater creatures down the toilet. He only needed one human eyeball for the spell to work, but figured using six fish eyes would more than make up for not using a human eye.

"I call upon you, Benzonah the Insidious. Demon of all demons. Demon of the seven hells, causer of chaos and destruction. I call upon you to do my bidding. To make all my desires come true. You will serve as my slave until my bidding is done. Then I shall return you to your home."

Barry picked up the goblet and brought it to his lips. He paused, thinking about what he was about to do. He wasn't worried about calling a demon to the world—well, truth be told, he was a little concerned—but he was more bothered by how horrible it was going to be when he drank the blood soup. He'd let the fish eyes go down like pills, as the spell required, and he was glad, because there was no way he was chewing them.

Damn, he was one desperate kid.

But he was tired of being a loser. He wanted to be popular, and to get the girl of his dreams—Suzy Sparks. He wanted her to love him.

His stomach churned and he felt nauseous. He wondered if this half-brained ritual would work. Maybe someone had put it online as a joke.

But he had to try something—anything. He was tired of getting picked on, of the name calling and physical abuse. Half of the kids in school knew him as "douche bag" and "dickhead" as well as other derogatory names given to him by Mike Schumacher and the rest of his crew. He was tired of whacking off all the time, and wanted the real thing. There wasn't a single female interested in him, not even the skanks or dweebs. He was invisible to almost everyone, except the teachers and bullies. The ridicule, the wedgies, the lack of female companionship—it all needed to end.

There was a time when he would've been happy if any girl, even an ugly one, showed an interest in him. But no more. Now he wanted a new life. He wanted all the negative crap gone. High school was tough, but if there was a chance he could change his life, his status, then he had to try. If all he had to do was drink some rabbit blood with fish eyes in it, then so be it. And besides, didn't other cultures drink blood and eat fish eyes as a delicacy?

The ritual Barry was performing came from a book called, *Dealings with the Seven Levels of Hell*—roughly translated from Latin. Barry spent days searching the internet for something that would help him improve his life. Everything he found was bullshit—diet, exercise, penis implants, butt implants, ab-flexers, herbs to stimulate his brain power. Finally, through trial and error—mostly error— he seemed to have found one that showed promise. It wasn't like the others, which claimed to be *for real*, or *authentic*. No, this particular website was simple and private, allowing only persons who contacted the owner, and passed his questionnaire, the right to enter.

The website's owner called himself Obidon, and after a week's worth of back and forth emailing, Obidon agreed to send Barry a book on how to raise a demon. Obidon suggested that Barry call upon Benzonah, a wicked and powerful demon who ruled vast territories in the Seven Hells. The demon was to be feared and never crossed; it could never be allowed its freedom, or to be trusted; when summoned, it would obey its master while the current deal was in progress. Benzonah could and would change Barry's life, giving the boy all that he wanted.

Without further delay, Barry pinched his nose, having decided to go forth with his plan. He closed his eyes and downed the contents, upending the goblet and making sure to get the last red drop. He swallowed the fish eyes whole, as the spell said they were not to be broken.

Releasing his nose, he placed the goblet on the ground; and wiped the excess blood from around his mouth and chin, then realized letting go of his nose was a bad idea as his mouth flooded with the horrendous taste of old pennies and rust. His stomach churned. He doubled over, fighting against the desire to vomit. Oh, how he longed for the cold tiles of his bathroom floor.

An hour later, he'd managed to keep himself from puking, but he was passing the worst gas he'd ever smelled. He wondered if his pants would ever smell fresh again regardless of how often his mother washed them.

Benzonah was a no-show. Barry assumed the demon would appear in front of him, awaiting its master's commands. Come to think of it, he really wasn't sure where the demon would appear. He should've studied the material for the spell more closely. He'd always been a slacker when it came to reading; skimming and reading the first line of every paragraph was usually good enough. He was sure he'd read that Benzonah would appear wherever he performed the spell.

After another hour of waiting, he stood. He was a fool. Duped by another bully, and one he never met or saw—some internet nerd getting his rocks off by knowing some idiot like himself was drinking eyeballs and rabbit blood. It was *back to his pathetic life*—as long as he didn't die from some disease the rabbit's blood might've had. Shit, he knew ingesting raw meat was dangerous, but what about blood? *Animal* blood? He'd been so stupid. Seeing the goblet lying in front of him, he felt a kernel of anger grow within himself. *Take it out on the fancy cup,* he thought.

Barry reared back to kick it, when a sharp, stabbing pain struck his abdomen. He bent over, clutching his stomach. He'd never been stabbed by a knife—save the time he sliced his fingertip while whittling wood on a camping trip—but it sure felt like someone was dragging a blade along his intestinal walls. He cried out, unable to straighten. Then as fast as the pain came on, it left. Barry breathed a sigh of relief and went to stand when the stabbing began again. A few moments later it stopped. This happened over the next few minutes, but to Barry it seemed like forever.

Damn it, he thought. The rabbit blood and fish eyes were killing him. All he wanted to do was make it to his house, but every step he took, he doubled over in agony. Finally, the pain stopped for more than a few moments. He didn't dare move, expecting his gut to act up, but after a while, nothing happened. He was sweating, his t-shirt soaked with perspiration.

He stood upright, then took a step and felt immense pressure in his stomach, but no pain, as if something had expanded inside him.

That's it. He needed to get home and have his

parents take him to a hospital. The massive pressure he'd felt in his gut moved downward and soon he was clenching his ass cheeks to keep himself from shitting.

Relief flooded through him. He thought he was dying, but it turned out he only had to crap. There was no way he was making it home without filling his underwear, so he unbuckled his belt and yanked down his pants—his bodily waste was at the end of the production line.

Unable to hold it back, he released his hold on his sphincter and let the excrement fly, but nothing came out. Red-faced and panicked, Barry pushed with all he had, fearing he might blow out his asshole or pop a blood vessel in his brain and be found dead in the woods, ass and pecker showing. He could see the headline now: "Local Boy Dies While Trying to Take the Biggest, Meanest Shit of His Life."

Barry would have laughed if he wasn't so frightened. It didn't make any sense. He knew what it felt like to have to shit immediately, but this was it tenfold. The pressure in his colon was overbearing and he feared his insides might explode if he didn't get the shit out. He pushed, holding his breath. His vision went static-like and he felt lightheaded, but kept pushing. If women could give birth, then he could shit, no matter how large the shit was.

Then, he felt his asshole ripping.

The pain was like nothing he experienced before, like someone had shoved his mom's curling iron up his ass. Barry wasn't about to go down without a fight, no matter how much angst he endured. He took in two lungfulls of air and pushed one more time, grunting like a woman giving birth to a super-sized baby.

Pain exploded in his rear, but he succeeded, feeling the fecal matter leave his body, flowing like a fire hydrant on a hot summer day. His insides deflated, body pressure returning to normal.

Done, his stomach felt vacant. It hurt to breathe, but the pain was nothing compared to how his asshole felt as it screamed at him for ice. He remained in the squat position, unable to move, wincing as his asshole throbbed.

He hoped he wasn't going to get hemorrhoids. His mother had told him people got them from pushing too hard. He was too young to have to deal with the annoying things. From now on he would make sure he ate a bran muffin every morning.

Damn, he could feel it. His asshole, cheeks too, were caked in the brown stuff. There were plenty of leaves around, but he'd need a whole tree to get himself clean. That was if he could even wipe. Just the thought of even the softest toilet paper touching down there was awful. Tiny green leaves would take forever and surely, he'd get plenty on his fingers.

Then he had an idea: he could use the rabbit. That would remove a lot of the larger stuff, the chunks, leaving only a thin smear here and there. He would use his underwear to clean up the rest, at least enough to make the trek home tolerable. Once the shit dried it would irritate the skin. The chafing would suck, and as soon as he arrived home, he'd pour a whole bottle of alcohol over his bottom to disinfect whatever might've been lurking on the rabbit's fur.

Barry's face wrinkled as the most horrendous odor he'd ever smelled struck his nostrils, like the time Billy

Higgins, the meanest bully in town, jammed Barry's head into a port-a-potty hole and wouldn't let him up until he stopped puking. It had taken him a week to convince himself that the odor wasn't permanently tattooed into his skin. Barry was grateful when the asshole moved.

Gagging, he quickly breathed through his mouth. Smelling other people's shit was nasty, like he imagined it was for most folks, but his own never bothered him. He could sit on the pot for hours, letting a huge dump rest below him, the excrement's odor saturating the air he breathed while he read from one of his mother's Cosmopolitan or father's Reader's Digest magazines, both periodicals overflowing in the magazine rack.

He guessed that most people didn't mind the smell of their own shit. As if the human body was okay with it, which made sense to Barry, otherwise people would be

17

vomiting almost every time they went to the bathroom. And the reason people didn't like other people's shit was because shit was filled with all sorts of dangerous bacteria, so the smell made sure people stayed away. That all made sense, but what didn't make sense was the fact that his own shit was making him want to hurl.

His asshole was starting to cool off, but it still ached. He needed to wait a little longer before he wiped.

He always liked to look at his shit. Well, he didn't exactly "like" or "enjoy" looking at it. No, it was more like a natural reaction, similar to moving out of the way when someone threw a rock at him. He imagined most people looked into the bowl after they finished, or at least as it circled the porcelain during a flush. It was just human nature; and the way this one felt and smelled he had to get a look at it. The damn thing must be huge.

Reaching down and grabbing his underwear and pants, Barry pulled them forward to avoid possible drippings when he moved, and turned around to get a look. His eyes bulged from their sockets as he stared at the fecal log. The shit was the size of his fucking forearm, the ground around it resembling a small tar pit. Then he noticed the spattering of some of his waste on the backs of his sneakers and pants. Damn!

He looked at the monster that caused all this, including his pain. Long and thick, it resembled a giant slug. Panic seized him when he saw streaks of red mixed within the brown slop. Blood!—he was bleeding. The shit had torn up his insides. Ripped his asshole wide open. He would have hemorrhoids for certain. His father once had the nasty buggers, the things so bad the man had to have surgery to remove them.

19

Barry shuddered at the thought of having a team of doctors stare at his bare ass as the roids were lanced off.

Needing something to blame, angry at his ass ruination, Barry stared at the shit, and flinched when it moved.

Unsure of what he had seen, he peered at the turd.

It moved again.

Barry blinked. Shits didn't move on their own. He figured the thing was just settling, like how a turd in the toilet bobbed and floated sometimes.

The turd moved again, this time wiggling like an insect in a pupa.

Barry leaned toward it, wanting a better look. A slit

formed at one end, then opened. A coughing sound emanated from it, like when a baby first breathes life. Spittle came from the orifice, dotting Barry's face in shit speckles.

Normally, if Barry had gotten shit on his face, he'd be grossed out and probably wipe at it and throw up from the smell, but he was too fascinated with what he was seeing. Something in his shit was alive!

Half an inch above where the mouth—was it a mouth?—had formed, two red slits appeared. *Eyes*, Barry thought. *The damn thing has eyes*.

Barry was going out of his mind. Somehow, the fish eyes, mixed with the rabbit blood, must have affected his brain with power equivalent to LSD. He'd smoked pot before, but had never taken acid, although imagined he was experiencing an acid-trip. Unworldly things, like flying bed monsters, talking forest animals, and turds that came to life had to be part of his tripping.

Thinking he may have overdosed on rabbit blood and fish eyes, Barry took off for his house but forgot his pants were wrapped around his ankles. He tripped and fell on his face. He rolled over onto his back, lifted his legs up, grabbed his jeans, and wiggled into them, not caring that his shit-smeared ass just became messier. He'd clean himself up later, once he knew he'd be okay.

He sat up, ready to get to his feet, when he saw his turd spring from the ground and land on his chest, the force pushing him back to the ground.

A horrendous, nauseating stench, like the nasty breath of his third grade teacher, Mrs. Peeper, wafted into his nostrils. Barry wanted to scream but gagged instead. The turd was no longer just a turd, but some kind of *monster* turd. It glared at him with its narrow, glowing, red eyes. Its tiny mouth was lined with angular teeth. It pointed one of its clawed fingers at him. Some kind of garbled language came from its mouth, a lot of hissing and clicking sounds, but for some reason, Barry understood it.

Well of course you can, idiot, he thought. *It's your trip.*

The shit-creature grinned, its teeth menacing, then spoke to him. It wondered how he could doubt its existence, since he was the one who had summoned it.

"You're Benzonah, the demon?"

The creature nodded. It was here to do his bidding, to help him get revenge on those who had wronged him, and to get him the girl of his dreams.

"You can do that?"

23

The creature nodded.

"But how? You're a turd."

The creature growled and called him a stupid boy. Barry had fucked up, royally. He was supposed to let the stew sit in the bowl and allow Benzonah to form through one of the fish eyes.

But Barry had swallowed the entire offering.

The contents, including the fish eyes, were absorbed into him and turned into excrement, leaving Benzonah to be born of feces.

But the demon said it didn't care. It was out of its prison, out of Hell, and free to roam the land of living flesh. It would help Barry, and when it was done with the boy, it had secret plans of its own. Its unexpected form could have great advantages in its plan to take over the world.

CHAPTER 2

Barry went back to his house with Turd, the name he'd given the demon. The little shit didn't seem to like it, but it was what Barry had wanted, so Turd obliged. Barry laughed to himself after naming his shit. The name Turd made the demon seem less dangerous than 1it was, until he looked into its eyes, which were filled with hatred and malevolence. He needed to make sure to never forget how evil Turd was.

Barry had known calling a demon was not exactly a good thing to do. Hell, it was downright risky. Demons were evil, plain and simple. He'd never truly believed the ritual would work, and maybe it hadn't. Perhaps he was dreaming.

However, the prospect of being able to turn his life around far outweighed his fear. Summoning a hellion creature would be worth it in the end. No one would get seriously hurt, and the demon was under his control. He'd learned all this online.

Barry carried Turd back to the house, using the goblet. The demon was able to walk, but as a fresh piece of feces, the little guy would probably pick up all sorts of debris from twigs, leaves, seeds, pebbles, cigarette butts and who knows what else.

Turd also left tiny, but noticeable, foot prints behind, like smudges from a small dog's paws after coming in from the rain. Something would have to be done about that—booties maybe? Barry couldn't have shit all around the house. His mom would kill him.

Barry entered his house quietly, not wanting to

draw attention to himself. He smelled like shit, and it wasn't only Turd's aroma that was causing the hideous stench. He didn't hear his mom, and raced through the kitchen, then up the stairs to the bathroom, making sure to keep a hand over the goblet so Turd wouldn't fly out if he tripped.

Barry stripped off his clothes; his jeans were shit-smeared in the crotch and down the legs. His underwear—forget it, they were going into a plastic bag, then the trash. He rested the goblet on the sink and told Turd to sit still.

He hopped into the shower, taking his clothes and shoes with him. The fresh, hot water felt wonderful, quickly eating away at the fecal matter embedded in his clothes and on his body. Looking down at the tub, he could've sworn he was in the middle of a torrential downpour where the streets ran brown with muddy water. Chunks of shit floated to the drain, causing a blockage and a chocolaty pool to form. Using his heel, Barry mashed the fudge-like mound, breaking down and forcing the excrement through the small drainage holes.

Barry rinsed his clothes, starting with his jeans, spending a lot of time on them, the material stained through. His shirt was next, especially the lower back part. His socks were streaked with brown and his shoes were discolored too.

After cleaning the articles of clothing, he hung them on the shower door handle and tossed his shoes onto the tile floor, then proceeded to wash his balls and ass crack. Most of the larger stuff had loosened and fell off while he was washing his clothes.

When he was all done, he rinsed the bar of soap,

making sure to clean off any fecal residue that might've attached itself. His whole family used the same bar, and he didn't want them using a bar of fecal soap, though it might be funny.

Barry toweled off, and made sure there were no pieces or smears of shit anywhere around him. He saw some speckles on the tile floor and wiped them up using cleaner that contained bleach. When he was finished, he grabbed the goblet and went over to the bathroom door, cracked it open and listened. He made sure the hallway was clear, then dashed to his room.

Turd and the goblet were placed on a small dresser, next to his Third Grade soccer trophy. The demon asked Barry to pay attention, as there were a few things to set straight.

The first order of business was keeping Turd alive,

which meant making sure he remained moist. Turd was already showing signs of drying out, his rich, dark color fading in places. The light didn't glisten as it had when he was fresh. Eventually, Turd would dry out and crumble, the demon sent back to Hell.

"How am I supposed to keep that from happening?" Barry asked. "Pour water over you ever ten minutes?"

Turd shook his head and explained to Barry that he could last a day before any serious damage was done, as long as he wasn't baking under the sun. Outside a cool home, Turd wouldn't last long at all.

"I know," Barry said. "Have you seen how fast dog shit dries up on a hot sidewalk?"

Turd narrowed his eyes, and Barry felt the little shit's frustration.

"What?" Barry finally asked.

Turd went on to explain how he needed a safe, preferably dark, moist place to live. Somewhere he could recover from any damage and rebuild himself.

"So where is this place?" Barry asked, and when he heard Turd's answer, he didn't like it one bit. "No! No way!" Barry shook his head. "You're not going back in me."

Turd spat off a round of angry sounding words, lots of high-pitched clicks and gargles. It was too fast for Barry to understand, but he knew the shit was pissed.

"You're too big to go back inside," Barry said. "Do you know what you did to my asshole? Fucking hurt like hell. I'm probably going to have hemorrhoids—and at my age! I still don't know how I shit something as large as you." Barry waved his hands and shook his head again. "There's no way I'm letting you back in."

Turd sighed and explained that it wouldn't be difficult or hurt when he went back inside. The little demon shit was able to change his shape, elongating himself, widening and so forth, as long as he remained pliable. By softening himself up and thinning himself out, the demon would be able to easily slide into the tiniest of holes without losing too much of himself— Barry's asshole being one of those holes. Then, inside Barry, Turd would be able to reconstitute itself by adding more of Barry's waste to its body.

Barry stared at him, mouth agape. He was the one who had screwed up the summoning, so now he'd have to deal with whatever consequences came with it, and he didn't want to lose the demon. Sure, he could try and call another, but he felt better having Turd around than some larger, scarier demon. If Turd got out of hand, he'd simply squash him.

"Really?" Barry asked. "You can do all that, and it won't   hurt?"

Turd assured him of a pain-free entrance, though Barry might feel a little bloated.

"Okay, fine," Barry said, still not happy about it, but if it was too uncomfortable, he'd just shit the guy out. He thought for a moment, wondering why he still smelled shit after he'd cleaned himself up, then realized it was Turd. "Hey, do you realize how badly you stink? What're we going to do about that?"

Turd wasn't able to detect his own odor. Well, that wasn't quite correct. He could smell himself, but the odor didn't bother him. Since he was made of shit, his smell was natural. But the demon imagined how it might affect others with its smell. Unable to come up with a solution, Turd simply shrugged.

"At least when you're inside, you won't smell up my room, so there's that I guess."

Turd nodded.

"So, when do we begin?" Barry asked, wanting to get this whole shebang going.

Turd shook his head, explaining how he worked better alone. There was really nothing for Barry to do. Turd had his demonic powers, though much weaker than normal, and would go out tomorrow after a good night's rest. That's when Barry's life would start to change and he'd get what he asked for: revenge and the girl of his dreams.

"So, I don't have to do anything except keep you warm and safe?" Barry asked, kind of liking that he

35

wouldn't have to get his hands dirty, so to speak.

Turd nodded and smiled, his tiny, pointed teeth giving Barry the willies. It was time for Turd to rest.

"You want to go back inside now?"

Turd nodded.

"How do we," Barry swallowed hard, "do this, then?"

Turd told Barry not to worry. All would be well. He told Barry to start by taking his pants off, spread his cheeks and relax. The more relaxed his sphincter was, the easier this would be. Once Turd was inside, Barry could go to the bathroom and wipe his ass, as Turd said he'd smear a little going in.

Barry yanked his pants down, then squatted,

making sure he was wide open. He was nervous and felt the lump in his throat, like a stone. He placed the goblet with Turd inside beneath him, then felt a tickling against his anus as Turd entered, cool and snake-like.

Barry felt himself filling up, becoming bloated. The sensation only lasted half a minute. The fullness he was experiencing traveled through his lower abdominal area, then vanished.

With Turd inside, Barry grabbed some tissues and cleaned his rectum right there in his bedroom, not wanting to have to walk down the hall holding his ass cheeks apart so as not to smear Turd's remnants and have a bigger mess to clean up..

He pulled up his pants and stood. This whole thing was crazy. Part of him still wondered if he hadn't knocked himself out somewhere and was dreaming this whole thing. Either way, he was seeing this through. What did he have to lose? Worse case, he went back to being the loser he already was. Best case, he'd be cool and have Suzy Sparks, the hottest girl in school.

It was unnerving having a demon living in his bowels, let alone having his own shit crawl back inside his ass. Shit was supposed to stay out, not return from whence it came. Wasn't that dangerous? Shit was full of what the body didn't want. Was he toxifying himself? Was that even a real word? He wondered if he would get sick.

Stop it, man, he thought. *Turd knows what he's doing and he'd never harm you. You're his master.*

Needing to take his mind off his worries, Barry pressed the power button on his video game console, picked up the controller, and played *Kill Them All 5*, forgetting all about Turd for awhile while he killed the

evil grandmothers that were baking children.

CHAPTER 3

Barry awoke with cramping in his gut. He sat up, rubbed his tummy, and ran to the bathroom as the urge to defecate presented itself. He sat on the toilet, ready to release the monster within, when he remembered Turd.

Was the little guy coming out, or was he having a regular bowel movement? If it was Turd, he wondered what would happen if he shat him into the toilet. Dammit, he and the little demon had never discussed when and where it wanted to come out. They should've talked about a signal or something—like three quick cramps followed by two slow ones meant it was Turd. He supposed the demon would want to be shat onto the floor, not in the bowl, since all that water would probably soften him too much. Come to think of it, he wasn't looking forward to having to clean up every time Turd came out or went back in.

Screw it. If Turd was on his way, Barry would immediately scoop him out of the water before any damage could be done.

Barry sat and pushed, his ass still aching a bit from yesterday. Regardless of what Turd had told him, shitting the little guy out would hurt, but Barry would just have to grin and bear it, as his father always said when things got tough.

Finally, the shit arrived, exiting like chocolate mousse, or soft ice-cream from the machine. His raw ass stung for a moment.. He usually hated taking soft shits, as they were more annoying to wipe, sometimes

41

seeming endless, but this time he was grateful. And knowing how tender his asshole was, Barry wasn't even going to attempt a wiping. No way. Instead, he would just hop into the shower and rinse himself clean.

He heard the demon's garbled cries from below, yelling for Barry to pick him up before he started to break apart.

Barry kicked off his shorts and looked into the toilet. Turd was floating and waiting for him to help. Barry looked around for something to grab the little guy with. Finding nothing suitable for the task, he reached into the bowl, bare-handed, and picked up the smelly bastard.

Turd was warm, almost hot. Barry loosened his grip as his fingers made indentations. He ran to his room, set Turd into the goblet—which he'd cleaned, and promised he'd be right back.

After flushing the toilet, he used his shit-free hand and turned on the shower. The water was freezing cold; goose bumps popped up along his flesh. Finally, when the water warmed, he positioned his ass to the stream, spread his cheeks, and let the water do the work. The tub quickly turned muddy as large chunks fell. He held himself there for a few minutes, then soaped up and rinsed.

When he felt thoroughly clean, he went to the drain, stomped down anything that didn't make it through the holes, then washed his foot. He gave his asshole one quick wash with the bar of soap, then exited the shower, dried off, and went back to his room.

"Damn," he said aloud. "It smells like one giant fart in here."

Turd told Barry that it was time to begin, and that he was going out for the day, maybe even the night.

"Okay," Barry said, and carried Turd in his goblet to the front door.

CHAPTER 4

Benzonah was glad to be away from Barry. Of all the humans in the world, he had to be summoned an idiot kid who screwed up a simple ritual. The great, powerful, über-feared demon of the six levels of Hell was a turd, and as if the humiliation wasn't enough, he was named Turd. At least the demon still had his demonic powers, however diminished they were. Ugh!—and his body . . . weak beyond pathetic. The wrong move, too long without moisture, and the results would prove critical. On the plus side, as long as he kept himself moist, his form was renewable. Human flesh was not. *Pros and cons of the job*, Benzonah thought.

According to the laws of Hell, Benzonah had to obey Barry's commands. But the boy had been a moron,

45

giving the demon an opportunity to do as he wished. Barry hadn't given any direct commands. Turd knew the boy's desires, and knew to speak first and have the boy assume the demon was going to do exactly as he wanted. Breaking away from Barry before his work was done would send the demon back to Hell, and Turd had no idea how long it would be before another might summon him, so he decided to stick it out.

Benzonah would take care of the human's problems and flee before the boy banished him back to Hell. Barry wouldn't likely do such a thing because he didn't know the rules very well, but there was always the chance. As long as Barry didn't order the demon to return to him when all the tasks were complete, which he hadn't so far, Turd would be free to do as he pleased, and killing Barry would be at the top of the demon's list.

Using knowledge it had taken from Barry's mind, Turd made his way over to Mike Bohmer's house. Mike was a bully and had been picking on Barry since elementary school, doing everything from spitting on him, to punching him in the stomach for fun, to pulling down his pants in the hallway. Turd would've had high hopes for the Mike if he continued along his path and worked his way up to killing someone. Benzonah the Insidious could always use more underlings in Hell. But an order was an order.

Turd made sure to stay off the streets; the hot pavement was deadly. He also avoided the underneath of pine trees—the fallen needles would stick to him and cause issues—and of course, he remained out of sight. The demon traveled through the grass and used trees, bounding from branch to branch like a squirrel, picking

47

up some debris along the way, but overall, staying clean. It had taken the demon thirty minutes, and although he was still moist, he was beginning to dry out.

Peeking out from behind a small bush, Turd scanned the Bohmer property. With the way clear, the demon dashed across the lawn to the house, where a patch of ivy grew. Turd latched onto a line of the fast-growing plant, and climbed. The demon made it to a second-story window and stood on the ledge. Using its hands, it scooped out small pieces of itself and lathered fresh shit over the dried-out areas. Immediate relief fell over the demon.

In his current form, with the sun beating down, the demon needed to get inside fast. Calling upon its ethereal powers, the demon focused on thinning itself out to the width of a sheet of paper, then slid under the window.

Pain wracked its body as it tore against jagged parts of wood. It popped out the other side and stood between the glass and a screen. Looking at himself, Turd was littered with flecks of timber, a dead spider, and a fly, along with particles of dirt. He ate the spider and fly and picked off as much debris as possible. Calling upon his powers had somewhat drained the demon, the insects having supplied him with little sustenance. The demon was smaller in size now, having left some of himself smeared under the window.

Holding out a clawed finger, Turd slashed at the screen, creating a small opening for himself, and squeezed into the house.

Cool air blanketed the demon as it looked upon the room.

A king-sized bed, with an ornate headboard rested on one side of the pink-carpeted room. A large flat screen sat on the wall across from the bed. Dressers lined with jewelry boxes and necklace trees took up space along adjacent walls. Based on the knowledge he had taken from Barry, Turd guessed he was in the parents' bedroom.

The demon hopped off the windowsill, then raced across the carpet, leaving tiny dabs of fecal matter behind. When he reached the door, he thinned himself out, again, and rolled underneath it. On the other side, Turd reformed to his natural size, then ran down the hallway.

The demon came to a closed door with the words, *Mike's Room, Beware!!!!* on the door. Dammit. Turd was going to have to call upon his powers yet again. He thinned himself, rolled under the door and into Mike's room, losing some of himself underneath.

Turd reformed and was even smaller than when he left the parents' room. This soft, pliable body was very useful, but way too easily damaged. Turd would have to find a way to protect himself—like maybe wrapping himself in plastic, saran wrap, or a sandwich baggie. The demon would try out some of its ideas later.

The boy's room was messy, littered with clothes, stained paper plates, utensils with crusty food on them, and soda cans, not to mention magazines and other things. A computer hummed on a desk in the corner, the waste basket below overflowing with stiff tissues.

Movement from the bed caught the demon's attention. Turd dove inside a nearby sneaker—the odor horrendous—then poked his head out and saw that he wasn't in danger. To his pleasant surprise, a foot was hanging off the bed.

Mike was home and asleep.

The demon wondered why this was so, considering how most young lads enjoyed warm spring afternoons with their friends.

Turd ran across the carpet and climbed up the comforter that draped off the bed. The kid was facedown and wearing only boxers. The demon leaped over both of the boy's legs and crept up to his face. The pungent stench of alcohol wafted over Turd, and then he knew why the boy was fast asleep. The kid was hung-over.

Climbing onto Mike's lower back, the demon lifted the band on the boxers and slid between the ass cheeks. Using its demonic powers—not having much left in the tank—Turd softened and elongated himself, then slid into Mike's anus.

CHAPTER 5

Mike woke with a start. He pushed himself off his bed.

Standing, he looked around his room. Something wasn't right. It was as if he was looking out of the eyes of someone else. Relief flooded over him as he realized he had to be dreaming.

"Mike," his mother called from downstairs.

He walked over to the door and opened it.

"Mike," his mother repeated, her voice much louder now, "you awake yet?"

He tried answering her, but nothing came out of

his mouth. He tried speaking again, but nothing happened. Come to think of it, he couldn't move. He just stood in the doorway. His body wasn't his, and for the first time since he woke, he had the feeling that he wasn't dreaming.

You are mine, boy, a scratchy, cold-sounding voice said. *I, Benzonah the Insidious, demon of the seven levels of Hell, am in control of your body*.

Mike had smoked laced pot before, taken acid, even snorted coke once, but he'd never experienced anything like this. He couldn't look around the room because his neck wasn't responding to his wishes, but even if he could move he didn't think he'd see anyone around him. No, the voice had come from inside him.

Mike wished he was caught up in some strange nightmare, but everything was too vivid, too real. But he had to be asleep, unless he was sleepwalking or having some kind of seizure.

He tried screaming himself awake, but he remained silent. Then, he heard himself speak, though it was not because he had wanted to.

"Yeah, Mom, I'm up here," he heard himself say.

Mike attempted to move, to speak, to do anything to wake himself up, but nothing worked. He watched as he stepped into the hallway and headed down the stairs and into the kitchen. His mother was placing two grocery bags onto the counter.

"You look like shit," she said, shaking her head. "Get your ass out to the car and help me with the groceries."

Mike watched the view change to the set of steak

knives resting in the block of wood near the sink. He walked over to them, wrapped his fingers around the largest handle and removed the bladed implement. He felt himself smile, his cheeks pulling back his lips. He turned around and saw his mother crouched in front of the open refrigerator. She pulled a carton of orange juice out of the paper bag that rested on the floor.

Mike took two steps toward her.

She reached into the bag again and grabbed a head of lettuce, then placed it into the fridge. "Mike, why are you still here? I've got milk in the car. It's been there for thirty minutes. C'mon."

Mike felt his grip tighten around the knife's handle. Malevolent thoughts filled his mind. The scratchy voice said, *Kill. Kill. Kill.*

He started forward, fear squeezing his heart. He

wanted to scream and warn his mother, but no words came from his mouth. She needed to look at him. Know what he was going to do. Run. But it was as if he was watching from somewhere far away, just along for the ride.

His mother stood, slammed the door closed and glanced his way. "Mike," she said, confused. "What on earth—"

Mike's arm swung upward. The knife's blade plunged into his mother's stomach. She let out a gasp. Her eyes bulged from their sockets. She stared at him in shock and disbelief. He pulled the blade free and jabbed it in again, and again, and again, his insides burning with hate. At the same time, he screamed soundlessly in his own head, begging to be woken from this nightmare. He was holding her up with one arm, the knife still in her. Blood leaked from her mouth. Her head shook slowly, her eyes tearing. Then the light faded from those blue orbs and he knew she was dead. He let her fall to the floor, holding onto the knife. He stared at her corpse, its eyes open, and felt himself smile again.

Mike headed over to the table and sat in one of the chairs. Red surrounded his mother's body, the pool growing. He cried, cursed and pleaded, but it was all unheard by his own ears. Something evil had taken over his body, of this he had no doubt.

It took five hours before his father came home, announcing his arrival with a verbal shout to Mike's mom when he entered the house. Mike's view hadn't changed during the whole five hours, and he had to stare at his mother's dead body the entire time, feeling the evil within him enjoying every moment of his torment.

"Kelly?" his dad said. "You home?"

Mike hurried over to the kitchen doorway and waited off to the side, hugging the wall.

His father entered the kitchen, passing by Mike. The man stopped short. "Oh my—" The man's words were cut off as the knife's blade ran across his throat. Blood spewed forth like a geyser. Mike brought up a knee and kicked his father in the ass, sending him forward as he clutched at his throat. The man tripped over his wife's body and crashed to the floor.

Mike's father struggled to rise, but his hand slipped in his wife's blood, and he went face-first into the hard ceramic tile, the crunch of cartilage echoing in his ears.

Mike stood there watching his father thrash about. The man was a fighter. He turned over onto his back, revealing a glistening neck, chest, and face.

The slit across his throat was open like a dark eye, blood continuing to flow. The man reached out to Mike. He wanted his son's help, but then he yanked his hand back as his eyes settled on the blood-covered knife in Mike's hand. Recognition exploded across the man's face. He knew what his son had done.

"That's right, old man," Mike heard himself say. "I killed the bitch. And you're going next."

His father reached into his pants pocket and withdrew his cell phone. He was coughing up blood, gagging. The phone slipped from his bloody fingers and clattered to the floor.

Mike watched his father's body go limp, the fight gone from him. A few more gurgling breaths sounded, the blood bubbling around the slit. A look of absolute terror crossed his father's face, and then it was gone, replaced with a vacant look, eyes focusing on nothing. Mike knew the man was dead.

Mike called 911, but not of his own doing. Whatever was inside him had done it. He said, "I killed my parents," then gave his address and hung up.

He grabbed a bowl from one of the cabinets and scooped some his father's blood into it. Next, he pulled a small paring knife from the wood block and knelt beside his father, the blood soaking into his pants like warm syrup.

He jabbed the blade into his father's right eye socket and cut out the eyeball, before repeating the procedure to the left eye. He plopped them into his mouth, then brought the bowl of blood to his lips and drank.

With his work done, the demon put Mike's conscience to sleep and exited the kid's body through the anus.

Turd was recharged, reformed, back to his normal size.

With his blood-lust satiated, the demon left the house, knowing its brethren would soon arrive in Mike's large intestine. The kid would be arrested and taken to the police station. There, the demon would exit Mike and possess another by hiding in a toilet and jumping into an officer when he came to take a shit.

The demon summoning cycle would continue, and Turd's army would grow.

CHAPTER 6

Next on the demon's hit list was Brett "Ogre" Damshell, an oversized, mindless oaf and the real muscle behind the bullying group. He was on the football team, crushed soda cans against his forehead during lunch time, and belched the alphabet almost everyday.

Turd made his way over to the oaf's house, which was two blocks away from Mike's. The demon made sure to stay in the shadows of trees, cars, and whatnot, and avoided the freshly-mowed lawns. It took Turd ten minutes travel time. The little shit had leaped from a tree to a telephone pole and back to a tree again, the high-wire act a little unnerving.

Brett's father, Mark Damshell, was a notorious Sunday afternoon barbecuer and heavy drinker. He was a mean son-of-a-bitch, always hollering at this and that. The neighbors stopped complaining after Mr. Millburry's and Mrs. Weiner's car tires were slashed after they called the police to complain. Mark's brother was a member of the police force, and always made sure his brother stayed out of jail—the two equal when it came to asshole status.

Benzonah hated having to waste such a fine middle-aged and disgusting individual. Sure, the demon despised humans and wanted them all to suffer, but he'd rather have the dregs of society, the killers, the abusers, live, and be able to harm others. The more of them there were, the more Hell's army would grow.

Brett's sweat-dripping, ass-crack-showing father was washing his 1979 Mustang, listening to some rock and roll on the car's radio. The house's garage door was open. Turd made sure the coast was clear, then darted from tree to bush to tree again before he dove and rolled into the garage.

The demon was on his feet in moments, his back against the cinderblock wall. Some debris stuck to his body, but nothing worth worrying about. The garage floor was practically spotless, save a few old oil stains.

A door was located at the back of the garage. Turd hurried to it. A large gap existed between the bottom of the door and the floor. Cool air wafted outward. Turd knew air conditioning when he felt it. He didn't need to thin himself out much, and rolled under.

The demon found himself in a large living room with shiny wood floors. He dashed across the room and into a hallway. A set of stairs was ahead of him, next to a doorway that led into the kitchen. On his immediate right was a closed door.

Turd dashed forward into the kitchen, the cool tile floor refreshing. He didn't see anyone about, but noticed a pot on the stove with steam billowing from around the lid.

A toilet flushed from somewhere behind him, which meant the cook was done with their business and most likely coming back to check on the food.

Turd launched himself onto the counter where the stove was located. From there, he had a better view of the place.

The kitchen was divided in two. The stove, sink, and fridge were in one section, with a large opening in the wall which allowed a view of the kitchen/eating room. A swinging door, when closed, cut the rooms off from each other. Lucky for the little shit, the door was open.

Turd hopped down and ran into the eating room, fearing if he went back into the hallway, someone would spot him.

The eating room was bathed in bright sunlight. Two of the four walls were lined with large windows that supplied a view of the backyard and the forest in the distance. A table stood in front of Turd. He thought about hiding under the table, but the tabletop was made of clear glass. The demon could easily be spotted from above, and if the family had a dog, the demon would be in more trouble, as dogs loved positioning themselves under tables, and some were known to eat feces, though usually their own.

Looking to the right, Turd saw a small wicker love

seat sat in the far corner. A large, tropical, potted plant sat opposite it.

Needing to move quickly, Turd dashed over to the potted plant, slipping and sliding a little on the tile floor as he went. Somewhat hidden, he peered from around the ceramic pot, and saw that the table was set up for a meal; plates, cups, forks, and knives displayed before each of the four chairs.

Turd heard a door open and footsteps as someone entered the kitchen. He looked up and through the opening in the wall and saw a woman at the stove. She lifted the lid, brought her face close to the steam, and inhaled.

Turd crept out from behind the pot and made his way along the wall below the window opening to the swinging door. He ran through the doorway back into the kitchen and past the woman, who was facing the stove and stirring the contents of the pot.

Turd bounded up the stairs, hurried by a closed door with the words *Sally's Room* on it, finding Brett's room next, the door open.

The place was the complete opposite of Mike's. Everything was orderly and clean. Not a single article of clothing was on the floor. There were no dishes, soda cans, or garbage anywhere. Various sports trophies lined shelves along the wall above a dresser. The bed was neat, the comforter creased at the corners and even all the way around.

The big oaf was a neat freak!

With the boy obviously not home, Turd would have to wait. Impatience flowed through the demon like a tornado, but under the commands of a human, he would have to quell his displeasure. But time was of the essence. Turd needed to finish Barry's wishes before the kid found out what the demon was really up to. If that happened, the kid would probably panic and send Turd back to Hell.

So far, Turd hadn't gone against the kid's wishes. The demon hadn't killed Barry's targets, and the boy hadn't said anything about killing others. But if Barry found out, he was sure to send Turd back to Hell for that too.

Demons were devious creatures, and a person had to be very specific, making sure to cover all bases when dealing with them. Lucky for Benzonah, Barry was an idiot.

Turd hopped onto Brett's computer chair,

smudging a little of himself on the fabric, then climbed onto the desktop. A lamp, a block of sticky notes, and a few smaller trophies sat next to the computer monitor. A large trophy, containing a golden baseball player swinging a bat with the words "2012 MVP" engraved below it on a shiny blue plaque, sat on a shelf behind one of the computer's speakers. Turd climbed up, hid behind the award, and waited.

Having been inside Barry and having shared the kid's knowledge, the demon knew most teenagers were obsessed with checking their cell phones and computers, which was why the demon situated himself on the boy's desk. Turd hoped the human would sit before the computer and check email or Facebook before heading off to dinner.

Turd didn't have to wait long before Brett entered

his room. As the demon supposed, the large kid threw a duffel bag into his closet and went right to his computer.

He tapped the keyboard and the screen came to life. His face scrunched up, revealing a look of confusion. He sniffed the air, then pushed the chair back and looked at the bottom of each foot. Shrugging, he pulled the chair closer in and clicked his mouse, then tapped the keys on his keyboard. In moments, he was laughing his ass off, his mouth agape.

Using his demonic powers, the demon stepped from behind the trophy and concentrated on the boy's gaping orifice. Bending his little legs, Turd launched himself toward Brett's mouth like a missile.

*   *   *

Brett loved receiving jokes to his inbox from FunnyFuckers.com, a hilarious website dedicated to crude and slapstick humor, like someone falling down stairs, getting pied in the face, hit in the balls, as well as a plethora of other things. He laughed away, gulping in air to get another lungful of chuckle out, when something streaked through the air and entered his mouth, filling it completely.

Brett's head jerked back from the impact. He shoved his chair backward and attempted to spit out the soft object in his mouth. His tongue worked furiously to get the soft substance to the front, but the thing seemed to be fighting him. He'd never tasted anything so horrible, like raw sewage but in solid form. The acids in his stomach were already preparing themselves. He took a deep breath, allowing his olfactory senses to kick in big time, and then it hit him— and he knew he had shit in his mouth.

His mind must've been working furiously, because it went back to a few moments ago when he thought he smelled shit and realized that he had, but his brain was also confused, because he had no idea how this could be happening.

Screw that, who the hell cares how, it is happening!

He had shit in his mouth!

Shit!

It didn't make sense, unless someone had set up a booby trap, a nasty booby trap. But there's no way anyone in his family would have done this. None of that mattered now; he needed to get the crap out of his mouth.

Brett kept working his jaw and tongue, trying to spit the shit out, but he could've sworn the shit was not only fighting to stay in, but moving around, as if alive. He didn't want to use his fingers and get shit on them, but figured if it was in his mouth, having it on his fingers wouldn't be so bad.

He shoved his fore and middle fingers into his mouth, and suddenly the need to puke was overwhelming.

He bent over. His stomach muscles clenched, but nothing came up and the shit-thing was at the back of his throat.

He was going to swallow it!

Suddenly, he couldn't breathe, and his gag reflex failed.

*   *   *

Turd slid about the boy's mouth, using his powers to bend and twist around the immense pressure of Brett's tongue. He managed to crawl to the back of the throat and block off the air supply, stemming the kid's need to vomit.

Unable to breathe, the kid passed out and fell to the floor, landing hard, jolting Turd hard against a row of teeth.

Pushing against the jaw, Turd opened the kid's mouth and exited. He ran to Brett's waist, slid into his jeans, and then into his anus, leaving a smear like melted chocolate behind.

Inside the colon, warm and finding replacement parts, Turd focused his demonic powers and gained control of Brett's mind.

*   *   *

Brett slowly came to. He remembered what happened and shot to his feet. No, that wasn't right, because he was already standing. There was no way that had been a dream because his mouth tasted like shit, though he wondered how he was able to sleep standing up.

He tried moving, wanting to run to the bathroom and chug a bottle of mouthwash, but he found that he couldn't move. He figured he was having a stroke, that the shit wasn't a shit, but some kind of poison that had fucked him up mentally. Panic raced through his mind until he heard the voice.

The voice was cold and raspy, like a sick person's, but filled with malevolence. He'd heard voices like this, but only in movies. They were usually set for the villains.

Idiot boy, the voice said. *You are mine to play with. A sheep to be slaughtered, but first there is work to be done.*

The voice went on, letting Brett know there was no hope and that he was only a passenger along for the ride.

Brett watched himself go to his closet and take down the large case containing his compound bow, the tool he used for hunting deer. He placed the case on his bed, opened it, and removed the weapon. He felt himself grin as he eyed the five razor-tipped arrows attached just above the bow's grip. Brett pulled one of the arrows free and readied it for flight.

He exited his room, wondering where he was heading and what he was going to do. As he made his way down the hallway to the stairs, he told himself that he was dreaming. He had nothing to worry about. He didn't eat shit and he wasn't really doing anything but sleeping in his bed.

Feeling a little better, Brett was ready to settle in and see where all this was going when the voice spoke up, telling him that he wasn't dreaming and this was all real.

"Bullshit," Brett said, his voice sounding like it was trapped in a small space, deadening quickly.

The raspy voice laughed.

Brett entered the kitchen, stopping just inside the door. His mother, Barbara, was at the stove, scooping homemade mashed potatoes out of a pot. Looking through the opening in the wall, he saw his father sitting at the table, upending a beer can. Another one was set before him, its outer shell sparkling with perspiration.

Brett raised the bow, drew back the arrow, and took aim at his father through the opening in the wall. The man froze and slammed the empty can down hard onto the table, his face in a snarl. "What the hell are you doing, boy?"

Brett's mother turned and faced Brett. "Oh my God," she said, putting a hand to her mouth. "Put that down."

"Son," Brett's father said, shooting to his feet and sending the chair crashing into the wall behind him, "you just earned yourself a beating you'll not soon forget."

Brett wished for once his old man would back down, but the inability to believe someone like his son could harm him, combined with the alcohol, was too much. Brett knew his dad wouldn't flinch, thinking his son would never do what he was threatening. It was all just for show.

Brett screamed at his dad, telling him to get down, to hide. But it was too late. He released his fingers from the string. The arrow shot forth and struck the man in the neck, pinning him to the wall behind him.

Brett's mother screamed.

Brett felt the evil within him rejoice, the raspy voice congratulating him on the incredible shot. Surely the man would not die right away.

Brett's father clawed at his throat and grabbed the arrow as blood oozed from where the projectile had entered. He coughed up blood. His eyes bulged with fear and disbelief. The man's hands turned glossy-red as blood flowed over them. Finally, he locked eyes with Brett and the fear vanished from them, replaced with pure anger. The man tried to talk, but his larynx had an arrow through it, and he only wound up coughing up more blood.

Brett turned his attention to his mother. Her face was pale, mouth agape. She shook her head. "Stay . . . stay away from me," she said, pressing up against the sink.

Brett plucked another arrow from the arrow holder, readied it, then pointed the bow at his mother. She closed her eyes and put her head down. Brett turned toward his father and shot him in the chest. The man's body spasmed, then went limp, the arrows keeping him upright.

Brett looked at his mother and dropped the bow.

His mother flinched as it clacked to the floor.

He felt himself smile, then walked over to her. She opened her eyes and looked up at him. "No, no, no. Stay away from me."

"Shut the fuck up," he hollered and backhanded his mother across her face. She flew into the counter and crashed to the floor, hitting her head. Her eyes rolled up right before she went limp.

Brett headed over to his father's corpse and smeared some blood onto his fingers. On the wall next to his dad, he wrote, *The devil made me do it,* and wondered if that was true.

Using his fingers, he reached up and dug out one of his father's eyes. The task was gruesome, and he thought he would throw up and pass out, but the sensations proved to only be in his head. Next, he got out a bowl from the cabinet, held it under his father's neck, allowing blood to pool into it, then sat at the kitchen table, said some strange sounding words and consumed the eyeball, whole.

*   *   *

Turd used his ethereal powers to send the boy into

unconsciousness. He truly enjoyed his latest kill, and wished he could have killed the mother, slaughtered her slowly, taking pieces of her flesh a little at a time, but the demon needed her alive, at least for awhile. Turd should have left one of Mike's parents alive, using the vessel to spawn another demon soldier, but the blood lust had been too great, the need to kill overwhelming. He was satiated somewhat, and knew to leave Brett's mother alive.

With his work complete here, the demon shit himself out, knowing in less than an hour another of his brethren would arrive. Brett would then be killed, and his mother would be possessed, head to a neighbor's house and repeat the summoning ritual, calling another demon from Hell.

CHAPTER 7

Devin Fallan was next on the demon's hit list. It had taken Turd almost twenty minutes to reach the boy's home. He had managed to stay relatively clean, picking off what he could from his body. But to his dismay, he looked across the yard and saw that Devin was riding a lawn mower, the kid's frame bouncing up and down every time the machine hit a bump.

There was no way the demon could get close enough without possibly becoming embedded with cut grass, or worse, getting turned into lawn fertilizer.

Peering from under the lilac bush he was hiding within, Turd saw a shed, the doors open. Figuring that's where the mower was stored, the demon bolted from his cover and scampered across the hot driveway, jumping over the cobblestone brick lining that ran along it and up to the shed.

Turd was gooey by the time he reached his destination, his form slick from the sun's shining rays. A number of grass strands were stuck to him. He peeled them off and left them in a pile next to a rake.

The shed's interior was sweltering, like some kind of jungle death box where prisoners of war were held. But it was perfect for the demon, his body loosening up and remaining moist longer in such an environment. Sure, his form wasn't as solid, but he didn't have to worry about drying out as fast.

Looking up at the walls, he saw hedge clippers, a chainsaw, a weed whacker, and a sickle. A gas can sat in the far corner. Next to it was a push mower. The demon rubbed its claws together in glee. The place was a playground for disaster, the potential for bloodshed and painful death incredible.

The demon climbed up onto a table at the rear of the shed, then worked his way up to the roof where plastic ledges came together and worked his way over to the doors, where he waited.

An hour later the shed rumbled, and Benzonah heard the mower's engine growing louder, the machine returning to its place of slumber. Turd readied himself to pounce on Devin when the kid pulled the mower inside, but then he heard the engine sputter to a halt just outside the shed. Maybe the kid wasn't finished with the yard work and needed different equipment.

Turd waited, ready.

Devin entered the shed. He wiped his forehead

with a rag, then tucked it into his back pocket. He went over to the wall of tools and grabbed the weed whacker.

Feeling the time was right to attack, Turd jumped down and landed on Devin's head with the splat of a gooey piece of fudge. One of his claws broke off and bounced to the floor. The demon had underestimated the heat index inside the shed—his form softer than he anticipated.

Devin screamed and dropped the weed whacker.

Benzonah called upon his demonic powers to harden himself.

Devin pawed at his head. Turd tried dancing out of the way but ran into the other hand. The boy wrapped his fingers around the demon and squeezed. Turd fought against the attack with his demonic powers of hardening, but it was no use; the kid's grasp was too strong. A moment later, Turd found himself in front of the kid's face, staring up at a disgusted and confused-looking Devin.

Turd closed his eyes and mouth, camouflaging himself so he appeared to be a regular piece of shit.

"It can't be . . ." the boy said, then brought Turd closer to his face and sniffed. "Aww, crap!" he shouted.

Turd opened his eyes. The kid's grip had loosened, his face scrunched into a grimace. The demon swiped out with his clawed hand, tearing into the kid's nose, leaving fecal residue in the gash, something sure to become infected. Devin shouted in pain and surprise, his mouth opening wide. Turd reacted instantly, and calling upon his ethereal powers, launched himself at the gaping maw.

The demon was halfway into the kid's mouth before he felt teeth slice into his soft flesh. Pain shot through him as his lower half was severed.

Turd felt the power drain from him, weakness settling in. The demon's only hope at survival was to reach the kid's large intestine, but Turd wondered if there was enough of himself to block the kid's airway and knock him out.

The kid's tongue worked feverishly to push out the demon. Turd saw the throat muscles working, the gag reflex coming. The demon would be pushed out by vomit if he didn't act fast.

Turd sank his claws into the kid's tongue and pulled himself along to the back of the throat. He lashed out, slicing up the inner cheek flesh, inflicting as much pain as possible to distract the boy's body from feeling nauseous.

Turd reached the back of Devin's throat and swiped his claws at the kid's uvula, severing the teardrop-looking piece of flesh. Regardless of his efforts, the kid was bent over, ready to hurl. Panicked, the demon called upon his remaining powers and shot forward, hoping to cut off the kid's airway and knock him out, but being smaller than usual, he wound up shooting down the trachea like a jet-propelled rocket and landed in the stomach with a splash. The sound of acid sizzling echoed in the small chamber, the corrosive liquid immediately melting the demon's soft shit-flesh away, like oozing streams of a chocolate candy bar left too long on the hot pavement.

Thinking quickly, seeing his claws crumble away,

the demon found the entrance to the stomach and entered the large intestine. He moved speedily along the spongy tunnel, rubbing himself along the walls to remove any acid that might still be present.

Finally, the erosion of his shit-flesh stopped. Relief flooded through the demon, but he was now a quarter of his normal size, and with lower half.

Turd pulled himself along, working tirelessly, not giving up, until he arrived upon a section of fecal matter. Like a pig in shit he rolled around, reconstructing himself back together. Smear after smear he grew, regaining his body, legs, and strength. He called upon his master in Hell, the devil himself, and asked for an immediate replenishment of demonic powers, because waiting for them to recharge on their own would take too long.

Turd was granted his wish, but along with it a warning that if the demon failed, he would be sentenced to a millennia of extreme torment.

Within moments, Turd was recharged. He released his spirit, and temporarily gained control over his host's mind.

CHAPTER 8

Devin could not believe what had just happened. He was baffled, frightened, and nauseous. A thing . . . a thing covered in shit had attacked him; jumped into his mouth and . . . And what? Slithered down his throat? Impossible, yet his mouth tasted awful, like—well, like nothing he'd ever tasted before. But the odor of feces was powerful. The word circling his mind was, *vile*, as if he'd eaten something no human was meant to eat.

He'd tried spitting it out, but it clung onto him, hurting him with its . . . claws? His mouth was on fire, burning with pain. He looked down and saw a part of the thing that had attacked him, along with droplets of red—his blood.

His eyes focused on the bitten-in-half thing. That's right, he'd bitten it, felt his teeth go through it, like when he'd eaten the finest Belgian Fudge. He bent forward, getting a closer view, and mashed it with his foot. A waft of shit-filled air fell over him, and then he knew it was definitely a piece of shit.

Devin bolted from the shed, screaming his lungs out. He stopped when he hit the lawn, bent over and puked. He hoped to see the other half of the turd on the ground, but it wasn't there. He took off running, tasting the blood running down his gullet, preferring the taste of it over the crap. He stopped, realizing he needed to keep puking until the shit came out.

Opening his mouth as wide as possible, Devin crammed two fingers down his throat—having watched his sister do it repeatedly—and forced himself to throw up. Pain wracked his core as stomach acid sizzled his wounds. Vomit spewed forth, a stream of reddish, tan liquid with chunks coming forth, but no half-eaten turd.

He was beginning to think that maybe he hadn't swallowed the turd, that maybe he had spit it out and the thing in the shed was all of it, but then his stomach cramped up. He hunched over, clenched his abdomen, and collapsed to the ground, the experience reminding him of the time when he was constipated. A rock-hard piece of shit had been working its way through his bowels. He wondered if the turd-thing had worked its way through his system and was inside his large intestine. No, impossible: his stomach acids would've dissolved it, or caused him to be sick.

He rolled back and forth, the pain white hot, and then it was over.

He sat up and got to his feet, readying for another

bout of angst, but none came. Something was definitely wrong and he should probably call 911. But what would he say—that a shit attacked him and was crawling around inside his gut?

Devin didn't care. He only wanted to get help. He'd worry about the repercussions later. He attempted to head to the house, but found he couldn't move. Then he heard a scratchy voice tell him that his body was no longer his. Looking ahead, he saw no one. Maybe someone was behind him? He felt his head move, his neck craning around painfully. He saw no one there, either.

Freaking out, wanting to piss himself, he walked to the shed, occasionally spitting blood on the way, all movements completely out of his control. Then, he realized what was going on. He was part of an alien invasion, the first of many to be taken over.

Unable to speak, he thought, *What're you doing,* hoping the alien inside of him would answer. *What do you want from us?*

The voice said that it wanted death and slaughter to all humans, to open the gates of Hell, and to sear the flesh off all living things.

That didn't sound like an alien. No, that sounded like something a demon would say, if such things existed. Devin continued to ask questions, but the voice didn't answer.

He entered the shed, his gaze immediately settling on the chainsaw hanging on the wall. He grabbed it, checked it for gas, and felt himself grin. He didn't like where this was going. He tried to gain control of his body, but it was no use.

The next thing Devin knew, he found himself standing in the hallway of his house. He pulled the chord on the chainsaw and the machine rumbled to life. He squeezed the trigger and the saw whined. Blue-colored smoke poured from the engine as gasoline mixed with oil.

His father hurried down the stairs, stopping just at the bottom. The man was shirtless, wearing only his boxers and black socks that ended just below his knees.

"What the hell is going on?" his father, Stan, yelled. He took a step forward and stopped, his face paling when Devin raised the saw and squeezed the trigger. "Shut that thing off, now."

Stan sidestepped into the hallway, arms up defensively. "I'm not sure what's going on, son, but please put that thing down."

Devin's mom came down the stairs, wearing a robe. "Devin?" she gasped, holding a hand to her chest. She turned to her husband. "What's happening, Stan?"

"Eeny," Devin said, pointing the saw at his mother. "Meenie," he said next, moving the blade to his father. "Miny," pointing the saw at his mother, ending with "Moe" and moving the saw to his father.

Stan must've seen something in his son's eyes, knowing that he was *it*. He flinched, spun and attempted to run, but wound up spinning his heels on the freshly-polished wood floor, like some cartoon character attempting to flee. For a nanosecond, Devin thought the scene was comical, but then the saw bit into his father's back, and all humor vanished. His mother's screams drowned out the whine of the saw's engine as it worked feverishly to chew his father's flesh.

Blood and bits of meat flew everywhere, caking Devin and the walls in gore. Devin felt the evil within grow excited, almost like a sexual orgasm. It loved the mayhem, pain, and bloodshed.

Stan fell to the floor and Devin continued to cut, slicing down the man's spine to his rear, connecting the incision to his father's ass crack. He sawed through to the floor. His father's body split open, held together only by the head.

Finished, Devin killed the saw's engine. The air was quiet. Too quiet. Where was his mother? Listening, he thought he heard her upstairs. He dropped the saw, the heavy machine making a squishy sound as it crashed onto his father's remains, and flew up the stairs.

He checked his parents' bedroom, then his own, the television and guest rooms, and, finally, the bathroom, but his mother was nowhere to be found. Then it dawned on him.

Devin ran back to his parents' room and threw open the closet door. His mother was cowering in the corner, her cell phone to her ear. Tears streamed down her face. "He's here," she said. "He's going to kill me."

"No, I'm not," Devin said. He reached down and yanked the phone from her grasp, and put it to his ear. "Tell the police that there's no need to rush. My father's already dead, and unless she does something careless, my mother will be fine. I'll be here waiting for the police, calmly." Devin took the phone away from his ear and tapped the *end call* button, then tossed the phone over his shoulder.

He reached out and grabbed his mother by her hair and pulled her from the closet. She wailed and fought, clawing at his hand.

"Shut the hell up, bitch," he said and put her in a
headlock and squeezed, cutting off the blood flow to
her brain until she passed out.

*   *   *

Turd knew the police would arrive soon. The
demon had wanted more time, but the situation was
what it was. He ran downstairs, popped out both of
Stan's eyeballs, gathered blood into a bowl and
performed the demon-summoning ritual, using only one
of Stan's eyes.

Sirens filled the fiend's ears as police cars arrived.
Turd knocked his host unconscious and shit himself out

after packing on more fecal matter. A new demon would be born within the boy. Mike would be arrested and join Mike Bohmer at the police station. Together, the two demons would summon other demons and cause chaos and destruction.

Turd slipped into Devin's mother's anus, woke her, and performed the ritual again, using Stan's other eye.

A few minutes later, another of Turd's brethren appeared, the newly-summoned demon arriving quickly. The new demon would play the part of a grieving mother. Then when the police left, it would have the mother head next door. There, it would knock out the missus, Marge Henser, then slip into her anus and kill Devin's mother, using one of her eyes and her blood to call another demon. This would continue on throughout the day and night, each new demon creating another, their numbers multiplying quickly.

Turd was more than satisfied that his plan was coming to fruition. He bid his brethren *adieu*, and exited the woman. His next stop would be Suzy Spark's house, the girl of Barry's dreams.

CHAPTER 9

When Turd arrived at Suzy's house, the demon was covered in roadside pebbles and forest debris. After picking himself clean, Turd climbed the telephone pole at the end of the driveway. He wasn't too keen on traveling along such a thin line, worrying about falling and the possibility of a large bird coming along and swooping him up.

He proceeded with caution, keeping an eye on the sky and his claws on the wire. When he made it to the house, he hopped onto a window ledge and breathed a sigh of relief. The little guy just wanted to get this last part over with and deliver the girl.

Ready to slash the screen, Turd paused after hearing a dog bark from within the home. *Shit*, he thought, then shrugged, sliced the mesh, and entered.

Looking around, he saw that he was in a bathroom. The demon hopped down onto the toilet seat, leaving a smudge, then onto the baby blue tile floor. He ran past the seashell-decorated shower curtain and over to the open doorway. He looked left and saw the hallway was clear, then looked right and saw the canine approaching, its tongue wagging back and forth as it panted.

Sifting through the memories of his former hosts, the demon knew the creature was called a pug, a small dog with a pushed-in face and bulging, wandering eyes. Deciding the best course of action, Turd tucked in his arms and legs and fell over, acting like a normal piece of shit.

109

The pug came over and sniffed the demon, then licked him, the rough tongue removing a thin layer of shit-flesh. From his vast array of human knowledge, the demon knew that dogs ate their own shit, but he had no idea if a dog would consume human feces. Then, as if answering his question, the dog opened its mouth to ingest the shit.

Turd sprung into action, jumping up with his claws and slicing the dog's snout. The animal yelped and took off down the hallway.

Not knowing how long he would have, the demon searched for Suzy's room, finding it quickly by spotting the girly décor—a bright purple-flowered bed sheet, pink-stickered computer, posters of boy bands, bottles of perfume resting along a dresser like dominos ready to get knocked over, and bikini panties hanging from the back of a computer chair.

Turd entered the room and saw that Suzy wasn't home. It was getting late, too. The demon would simply stay here for the night and have the girl jump Barry's bones tomorrow, fulfilling the contract between him and the boy.

Turd hid under the girl's bed. She came home a few hours later, talked on her phone, spent time on her computer, then finally went to sleep. The demon climbed up the comforter, slid under the sheets and worked his way over to her crotch. Calling upon his demonic powers, Turd turned himself into sludge and slipped into Suzy's anus.

CHAPTER 10

Brett awoke on the kitchen floor, confused. He had no idea how he arrived there. He sat up and leaned against the wall. The last thing he remembered was . . . his really fucked-up dream. He'd been locked in his own body, unable to control himself. He'd used his compound bow to kill his father. His ass felt . . . raw. He smelled shit, and wondered if he'd pooped his pants.

Brett got to his feet. Something wasn't right. Hesitantly, he sauntered over to the stove and peered into the eating room. His breath caught in his throat. His father was dead, pinned to the wall, just like in his dream, although now he knew it hadn't been a dream.

The room spun and his stomach churned. Nausea filled him. He turned and shot to the sink where he vomited, and remained in that position for awhile, as drool fell from his lips. This can't be real. He had to be dreaming. Reaching out, he turned on the cold water, rinsed his mouth, and washed his face.

Maybe he'd snapped. His father was a nasty man, a drunk who beat him and his mother on a weekly basis. The guy was an asshole and deserved what he got in life. But killing him was a bit much. And Brett didn't deserve to go to jail.

Brett had heard of people blacking out, not remembering what they had done, but he remembered everything—and the scariest thing of all was that he had had absolutely no control over what he had been doing.

113

He thought of his mother, wondering where she was. He remembered hitting her, then not much else.

"Hello, son," a voice said from behind him.

Brett spun around and almost collided with his mother. He could smell the coffee on her breath.

"Mom," Brett said, wanting to wrap his arms around her but not sure what to do. He wondered if she'd called the cops.

"Son," she said, which was odd, because she never used that word, ever. She always called him by his name.

A sharp, stabbing pain exploded in Brett's abdomen. He hunched over, unable to breathe, and saw a kitchen knife protruding from his gut, his mother's hand holding the handle.

"Sorry, sonny," she said, "but you're of no use to us anymore. The demon that grew inside of you is free, and is probably inside the neighbor by now."

Brett collapsed to the floor, the knife still protruding from his abdomen. He felt cold, as if the tile floor was refrigerated. Numbness set in quickly, and the last thing he saw was his mother's wicked smile as she waved goodbye.

David Bernstein

CHAPTER 11

Barbara watched the life leave her son's eyes. She was already numb with shock, but the weight of seeing both her loved ones dead was too much. Something bad had happened in her household. First, her son had flipped out, shot arrows into her husband, and then she lost control. Though she'd claim insanity, she'd never forgive herself. Once the shock wore off, she'd most likely spiral downward until she attained the nerve to kill herself.

Having witnessed her son kill her husband must've caused her to flip out, and in such a way where she lost control—literally. She'd had a psychotic break, her evil side taking over. The demonic voice she'd heard was

116

her own. She surprised herself at how easily she was able to think clearly about everything, making her break even scarier. The next step was to call the authorities and . . .

Barbara bent and pulled the knife out of her son's stomach. Apparently, she wasn't done yet. Control was out of her hands, so she acted like she was on a ride and watched, but then the ride grew too gruesome and panic set in; true, gut-wrenching, system-frying panic and torment.

Using the knife, she cut out her son's eyes and gathered his blood in one of the cereal bowls. Then, to her further dismay, she drank the solution after chanting some kind of gobbledygook.

If she hadn't been crazy before, at least in the eyes of a court, she would be now. She screamed and

117

screamed inside herself, then laid on the floor and fell into darkness.

*   *   *

The demon that Turd had summoned shit itself out of Barbara, making room for its brethren to arrive. It left the house and headed to a neighbor two houses away where it would possess another human, call more demons, and shed more blood.

CHAPTER 12

Suzy had no idea how she arrived at her current location. One minute she was fast asleep in her bed, and the next she was in what could only be Barry Gilbert's room, standing in front of the kid himself. He was staring at her with a disgusted look on his face, then covered his nose and mouth with his hand.

"What the hell is going on, Barry?" she asked, unnerved. "What the hell am I doing here?" She took a step forward, angry, ready to grab Barry by his hair, but felt a warm, gooey sensation in her pants. Then the horrendous stench of shit drifted into her nostrils. No, she couldn't have. She paused, and clenched her butt cheeks just to make sure. Then she knew—she'd shit herself in front of Barry Gilbert!

Forget how she got here, she'd deal with that later. For now, she had more pressing matters. "Bathroom, now!" she demanded.

Holding his nose, Barry said, "Down the hall, second door on the right."

Suzy did an awkward about-face and walked stiff-legged out of his room and down the hall to the bathroom.

She placed her cell phone on the sink, stepped into the shower and removed her shirt and bra, then reached out and placed those items on top of her cell phone. Suzy cringed at what she had to do next. She unbuttoned her jeans and slid them down. With the barrier removed, the stench worsened, and her need to vomit grew. She breathed through her mouth, seeing the dark stains on the insides of her pant legs. She was ready to turn on the shower and rinse her clothes when she felt movement in her panties. She froze. It was just the waste settling as she moved. Then, she felt it again, something wiggling, pushing against her flesh.

Freaked, Suzy yelped and flew out of the shower and over to the toilet where she squatted, making sure not to sit—the backs of her legs were smeared with shit and she didn't want to get any on the seat—and pulled down her panties, emptying the load within. She heard a splash below, then wiggled her rump to make sure the larger pieces fell off.

She squatted there for a moment, afraid to look, but she had to. There had been so much, more than usual. The laxative she'd taken before bed had done its job.

She turned around and glanced into the bowl.

Among the brown refuse and floating chocolate islands was a huge land mass, a piece of shit so large she wondered why her asshole wasn't searing with pain. Then, the shit moved and she flinched. Two red slits appeared, and she knew that she was looking at a pair of eyes. Below the eyes, a mouth formed, and the shit-thing grinned, showing tiny, sharp teeth. The thing growled. Suzy recoiled. She screamed and slammed the lid down, then pushed the handle and flushed the shit away.

*   *   *

Benzonah had no idea what went wrong. One minute he had been in control of the girl, ready to

deliver her to Barry and fulfill his contract, then WHAM!
he was flushed out of her like some regular piece of
shit. The intestinal walls rumbled, expanded and
contracted. Moments later, he was whisked away in a
flash flood and went sailing along the tunnel, like a kid
on a water slide. The rush of liquid was overpowering,
sending him out of her ass and into her soft panties
with a splat. The demon's shit-flesh was dissolving more
quickly than usual. The fiend searched his mind, and
then knew. The girl must've taken a laxative before she
came to bed. Turd hadn't been ready. Chunks of himself
had been blasted away by the rush of diarrhea and
eaten away by the chemical, making him soft. He could
do little more than lay against her ass, hoping his
strength would return soon.

Then, she had dumped him into the toilet and
flushed. If he'd had more time, he could've packed on

more waste, but as it was, the demon was fragile, losing pieces of himself and in danger of dying.

Turd flew through the pipes, tumbling and smashing against the steel. He grabbed whatever pieces of waste he could, trying to add a little substance to himself. But pieces of Turd kept ripping away. The demon was soft, so very pliable. If he didn't do something soon, his life would be over.

By the time he called upon his demonic power, Turd was the size of a peanut. He tucked himself into a ball and constructed an ethereal shield around himself. At such a small size, his powers were weak, but he managed to make himself as hard as a marble. Like this, he waited as he tumbled around the sewer system, praying to his dark lord that he be saved.

Sometime later, Turd stopped moving. He released

the shield and unballed himself. He was in some kind of chamber. He swam to the surface and looked around, seeing other debris floating about—soda cans, sheets of newspaper, toilet tissue, food, and of course, shit.

Making it over to a ledge, he pulled himself out of the water and rested for a few minutes.

Using the knowledge he'd acquired from his victims, he deduced that he was in some kind of sewage waiting room. Sunlight poured in from above at one corner. There were several other pipes leading into the room. At one end was a large, mesh-covered pipe leading out. Most of the chamber's trash was huddled against it.

Looking up, Turd realized he had a way out, but first he had to add a little substance to himself. Scanning the detritus, he found plenty of floating pieces of fecal matter, and of all colors, from green, to brown, to black and even red. Turd liked the idea of being multi-colored, like camouflage.

Using a Popsicle stick he found, Turd layered himself with the various pieces of shit until he was almost his normal size. The few pieces of undigested corn and seeds and whatnot he came across, he simply plucked off and tossed away. The process took a while, but eventually he was almost his normal size again. He grew stronger and felt better, his demonic powers returning.

A squeaking sound, like the chirp of a frightened bird, echoed throughout the chamber. It had come from one of the pipes. Turd peered across the room and into the pipe directly across from where he was standing, and saw two red dots. More squeaks came from the pipes. The red dots grew larger, and then Turd saw it: the large head of a rat. A moment later, another rodent appeared in another pipe. Soon, rats were pouring into the chamber from the pipes. And then Turd knew—the arrival of the latest batch of waste was like a dinner bell to the creatures. The demon was in no condition to take on an army of hungry, disease-ridden rats.

The beady-eyed animals splashed into the water, attacking every piece of edible debris in sight. Two landed on the small platform that Turd was standing on and charged at him.

Using his demonic powers, Turd squatted and launched himself into the air, just as the first rat arrived at his location. His powers weren't at their fullest, but he managed to just reach the ledge above. He grabbed hold and pulled himself upon it, then rolled over onto his back and sighed with relief. He'd come so close to being eaten alive.

Finally, he sat up and glanced down. The chamber was swarming with rodents, squeaking, fighting, and eating. He stood, saw the opening to the street only a few inches above his head, and pulled himself up.

He was free, standing at street level, hidden within the confines of the sewer grate entrance slit. The steel rectangular entrance was rusted and old, but kept the sun off his body. Outside, the day was bright. Turd could feel the heat coming off the pavement like a stove left on.

Testing how hot it really was, Turd stepped out for a moment and nearly lost his foot as the bottom melted away. Damn, he would have to move fast.

Across the badly cracked and sun-baked road was a

building, and in front of the building were grass, bushes, and trees, which meant shade. If he could make it there, he'd be okay.

Ready to run, the ground began to shake. Turd's body vibrated as a huge tire appeared, no less than a few feet away. An eighteen-wheeler's engine roared as it passed by, shaking a popcorn kernel free from Turd's back.

That was too close. Death was near. First the laxative, then the flushing, then the rats, the hot pavement, and now, if he'd moved without looking, he might've been flattened.

Turd didn't want to waste any more time. He was already beginning to dry in places and had to smear some of his slicker self over the drying spots. He stepped out, checked both ways, then darted across the road, his legs getting shorter as he went.

Turd made it to the grassy area in front of the large building and hid under an overgrown berry bush. He picked out a few leaves that stuck to him and was beginning to worry when he realized how free he truly was. He'd felt it after getting expelled from Suzy's anus. The contract had been fulfilled. Sure, the girl didn't do anything to Barry, but he'd done his part and delivered her.

The demon leaped with glee, banged his soft head into a sharp branch, then relaxed. Better yet, he'd managed to already start his army of fecal demons and kill a few people along the way. What more could a demon made of shit ask for? That was simple: world domination, turn the Earth into the cesspool it was, then unleash unholy hell upon it.

He and his army would work slowly. They'd take the town, then move on to the next one, multiplying like a plague, wreaking havoc and mayhem—and the stupid humans would never know what hit them.

Bringing himself back to reality, Turd surveyed his surroundings.

The demon was in some kind of industrial park. Another eighteen- wheeler drove by and headed down the street to one of the many factories that dotted the landscape. Black smoke billowed from tall chimneys. Almost all the buildings looked the same. They had square, with numerous tiny windows, some of which were broken out. Parking lots of the surrounding factories were either packed with cars or empty, making it easy to see which buildings were operational and which ones weren't. All along the road that led through the industrial park were sad-looking pine trees, clearly planted to try and make the ugly area more appealing.

Surveying the building behind him, seeing the empty parking lot on the side, Turd knew that the place was abandoned. The front gate had a *No Trespassing* sign plastered to it, and was chained together, preventing vehicles from entering the property. Windows along the upper level were smashed out. A sign reading, *Vestro Chemical Corp* identified the previous occupant, but it was sun-faded and peeling. A *For Sale* sign hung on the lawn, swaying gently as a warm breeze blew in.

Turd grinned as an idea came forth. The demon darted from his cover and ran alongside the building to the rear. He searched for a way inside, finding only locked doors and very high windows.

Making it to the loading bays around back, Turd

checked a few doors until he found an open one. Inside,

he explored, and eventually found what he was looking

for. The perfect place to raise his army.

CHAPTER 13

Barry wasn't sure what had happened. He'd been sitting in his room, about to play a video game, when Suzy Sparks walked into his room and shit herself. Turd must have come through, sent the girl over to get it on with him, or at least to talk. Her face had scrunched up, then he heard the wettest sounding fart he'd ever heard. Moments later, the room filled with the odor of shit. However, not just any shit, but the kind of shit a person took after a night of heavy drinking and eating greasy food. The kind of shit his father took after going out with his buddies.

He waited in his room, giving her time to clean up. *Ten minutes ought to do it*, he thought, then watched the clock take its time turning over the digits. Ten minutes seemed like an hour, worse than when he watched the clock in class.

Finally, he moseyed on down to the bathroom. He could smell the stench from outside the door, making the odor in his room seem pleasant. He pinched his nostrils shut, and knocked.

"Almost done," Suzy said.

"Need anything?" Barry asked.

"Could you get me a pair of pants?—sweat pants would be perfect."

"Sure," Barry said. He was glad to help, but she must've made quite a mess.

Barry ran to his room, deciding on which sweatpants to give her, wanting her to have the best, his favorite. He almost grew a hard-on thinking *his* pants would be on *her*, their groins having rested in the same place. He'd never wash them again.

He returned to the bathroom door and told her he had the sweatpants.

"Leave them," she said.

"Need anything else?"

"No."

"I'll be in my room."

Barry returned to his room but couldn't stay there for long. Though the odor wasn't as rank as it had been outside the bathroom door, it was still horrid. He wanted to ask Suzy to pass him the air freshener that was in the bathroom, but he didn't feel right about it, and besides, she needed it more than he did.

Barry remembered how much his mother liked candles and ran to her room. He went into her closet and grabbed one of the vanilla-scented candles—his mother's favorite—and returned to his room. He lit it using the lighter he kept in his junk drawer, then opened the windows, and carried the candle around the room, hoping to drive out the terrible odor.

With the smell dissipating, he put the candle on his dresser, leaving it lit, and sat on his bed. He thought about the events he'd just witnessed.

Suzy was hot, and even though she'd shit herself, he didn't think it'd stop him from wanting to be with her, including in bed. Sure, she'd be tarnished in his eyes, well, not tarnished, but not nearly as perfect as he'd thought. She was human. Hot girls didn't shit; it was a fact. At least that's how he imagined it. Who pictured hotties sitting on the pot, shitting last night's dinner? Peeing, sure, but not dropping a deuce.

Barry flinched at hearing the bathroom door creak open, as if Suzy was hesitant. He had no idea what to expect and straightened himself up, his heart racing.

Suzy stormed into the room, holding a small white trash bag, heavy with her soiled clothes.

"Give me your phone," she said, holding out her other hand.

"Why?"

"Because I dropped mine in the sink and it isn't working. I need to call the police."

"The police?" Barry said, taken aback. "Why?"

Suzy's eyes bored in on him. "I have no idea how I got here." She shook her head weakly. "I mean, you must've drugged me and kidnapped me, slipping me out through my bedroom window or something." She paused. "Did you kill my parents? Is that how you got me out of my house so easily?"

"No, of course not. I didn't kill or kidnap anyone."

She put a hand to her forehead. "I'm fucking hallucinating for Pete's sake. Seeing some weird shit."

Barry jumped off the bed. His voice was pleading. "I didn't kidnap you. I swear. You came here on your own."

"Bullshit," Suzy said, stomping her foot. "Now hand me your phone."

"And if I don't?"

Suzy locked eyes with him. She took a step forward. Barry swallowed. "I'll beat the shit out of you. Then I'll say you tried to rape me. Right now, it'll just be kidnapping, unless they find some kind of strange drug in my system, then I'll say you tried to rape me."

Barry pulled his cell phone from his pocket. "Look, if I *did* kidnap you, then why would I give you my phone?"

Suzy's brows knitted together. Her lips tightened into something resembling a sphincter. She appeared to be thinking. "Then what the hell am I doing here?"

Barry let out a breath and put his phone back in his pocket. "You wouldn't believe me if I told you."

"Try me."

Barry took a seat on the bed and told her to do the

same. The story he was about to tell her might be a bit much. She put her bag down and complied.

She listened as he spoke, not once opening her mouth to stop him. Her eyes went wide at times, then rolled at others. Barry told her the story of how he conjured Benzonah the Insidious, and how he did it incorrectly, creating a shit demon. Suzy's face paled during his telling. She held a hand over her C-cup-sized chest for most of the story. When he was finished, she spoke.

"You mean that thing that came out of me, that I dumped into the toilet, was this Benzonah, the demon you conjured?"

"What thing?" Barry asked, cocking his head.

"First," Suzy said, holding up a finger, "this whole situation never leaves the room. I'm beyond devastated. No one can ever know about this."

"The shitting-in-your-pants fiasco?" Barry asked, unsure if she meant coming over to his house, the shitting in her pants, or the demon.

"Yes. All of it." She threw up her arms. "Promise me you won't tell anyone about this."

"I swear," Barry said. "My lips are sealed.

Suzy closed her eyes and huffed. "I can't believe I'm about to talk to you about this, but . . . but . . . I could've sworn I felt something moving in my panties, you know after I . . ."

Barry nodded. "Go on."

Suzy opened her eyes and swallowed. Her hands were clenched together on her stomach. "I looked in the toilet after I dumped out the waste, and I swear my shit was looking at me. It even growled. I panicked and flushed it."

Barry's mouth dropped open. *No, it couldn't be . . . Turd?*

"What?" Suzy said, sounding worried. "It was the demon, wasn't it?"

Barry nodded slowly. "I think so. But it sounds like you killed it."

"Oh my God," Suzy said, standing, flailing her arms at her sides. "I don't know what's worse; the fact that I had a demon inside of me or that I had your shit inside me."

"Sorry," Barry said.

"Hey," Suzy said, catching his stare. "How the hell

did this all happen? I mean, how did I get involved with your demon?"

"Well, you see . . ."

"Spit it out, Gilbert."

"Look," Barry said, holding out his hands defensively. "I like you. I admit that. I mean, I really like you. I wanted you to like me so badly. And I hated Mike, Brett and Devin. I called the demon to help me get revenge on them, for all the mean things they did to me. And I wanted *the* girl, you. Turd said he could get you to like me. I had no idea he was going to possess you and force you to sleep with me."

"You fucking asshole!" she yelled and slapped him across the face.

"I'm sorry," he pleaded and took another blow

before cowering.

She stopped hitting him. "You had me possessed by a demon—a *fucking shit demon*?"

"I didn't know he'd be inside of you. Make you do things against your will. I thought he'd just tell me what to do to get your attention."

"You're a sad sack of shit, Barry. If I hadn't taken that laxative, who knows what I'd be doing—probably you." She shivered.

Barry took a step toward her and held out his arms.

She flinched and backed up. "Don't you fucking touch me."

"Calm down. Turd's gone. You killed him. He's nothing but mud-colored water by now."

Suzy stepped up to him. Barry held his ground, but

swallowed, getting ready to feel the impact of a punch to his gut or face. She poked him in the chest, hard. "If this whole mess wasn't so unbelievable, I'd have you thrown in jail."

Besides Barry's chest hurting from where she'd prodded him, he felt relieved that she wasn't going to involve the police. Suzy was right. No one would believe her, and if the truth got out as to her shitting herself in Barry's room she'd be ruined. Barry had blackmail material for life.

"I'm leaving," Suzy said. "But if I find out that you've sicked another demon on me, or tell anyone about any of this, I WILL KILL YOU!"

Barry was trembling, ready to piss himself.

"Got it?" she asked, smiling.

Barry nodded.

Suzy turned around, grabbed her soiled clothes and left.

From down the hallway, she said, "And I'm keeping the sweatpants."

Damn, they were his favorite pair.

CHAPTER 14

Barry was glad to be rid of Turd. He couldn't believe what the little shit-face had done. He'd been foolish, stupid, and crazy. And all to be popular and get revenge on the kids at school. He was just glad nothing really terrible had come of it. Especially now that he knew true evil existed. He would be changing his tune for good. Screw bullies everywhere. He was still young. He'd get a girl, eventually. If not in high school, then in college.

Yeah, it sucked being a semi-loner with few friends, a loser in the eyes of the popular kids, but weren't many of today's successful people once dweebs? Losers? Oddballs?

It wasn't like Barry was friendless. He had a few buds, close friends, and not just teammates or associates. They were losers like himself, but they were his people, and they enjoyed doing what he enjoyed doing.

Feeling better, he sat back on his bed and flicked on the TV, using the remote. He thumbed the channel button and surfed, looking for something to watch when he came across a "Breaking News" story. Highlighted at the top of the screen were the words GRUESOME MURDERS. A dark-haired woman holding a microphone was standing in front of a very familiar-looking driveway. Police cars and ambulances were scattered about the area, their flashing lights hypnotic. Barry turned up the volume.

The report was about two grisly murders that had taken place at Mike Bohmer's house. Both his parents were dead, Mike the alleged killer. Barry couldn't believe it. When the news lady finished her report, the broadcast switched to a different area of the town where another reporter was waiting to tell the story of another murder, this one at Devin Fallan's house. Devin had allegedly murdered his father. His mother was alive but distraught. The picture on the television switched to another locale, this one outside the town's police station. It was being reported that Mike and Devin were both dead, killed by police after they had stabbed two officers in the throat with a pen and a letter opener, killing them.

Barry felt trepidation building within, his mind on to something, but not quite there. But when the next news report came on detailing a third murder in his town, he didn't need to think anymore; he knew, *knew* that Turd had been the cause.

Barry pressed the power button on the remote and killed the TV. He sat for a moment, feeling numb, then sprung from his bed and ran down the hall and into the bathroom. He flipped up the toilet seat and puked his brains out.

When he was finished, he sat back against the cool tile wall, breathing in the ever-present lilac smell from when Suzy doused the place. He couldn't believe this was happening. He had specifically forbid Turd from killing the bullies, but the little shit had gone insane and killed their families. He had only wanted revenge, something to make those assholes realize they couldn't get away with being assholes. Maybe hurt them a little, turn them into losers. He never wanted them dead.

The only good news was that Turd was dead. Or

was he? He was supposed to banish him back to Hell when he was done with him, but since Turd was destroyed there was no need to . . . unless the demon had survived the flush. With its demonic powers, Barry supposed it was possible.

He jumped off the bed and sat at his computer. He logged into his email and sent Obidon a message, asking what happens to a demon if the host body is destroyed.

It seemed liked days passed before Barry received a reply, but it had only been a few hours, and came in the form of an instant message.

Obidon: *Has the demon fulfilled its contract?*

Barry wasn't sure. At first, he didn't think so, but then he thought about it. All the bullies were dead. Suzy had come to him. She was delivered.

BarryG123: *I think so. Yes.*

Obidon: *This is why it is important to follow directions EXACTLY—especially with demons. After the summoned entity finishes a contract, the summoner must complete the ritual and send the demon back to Hell. This should have been clear before you summoned it. If you did not do this, and it wasn't killed—which is hard to do—then you must track it down and destroy it.*

Barry decided to let Obidon in on his screw up, and messaged him how he had shit out the demon.

Obidon: *You're a fucking moron. Do you know that? You must. My suggestion to you: find your living shit and stomp it to death. Because if you don't it'll keep on killing and making more demons. A demon like the one you summoned is high up on the demon food chain. It has others that follow it. It will use the same ritual you performed to call others up from Hell and build an army. It will try to take over the world, bring Hell to Earth, because that's what most demons do, asshole. Good luck.*

Barry couldn't believe what he had read. Turd was building an army? He wondered what kind. An army of possessed people, or possessed turds? Obidon didn't respond to any more messages, including emails, so Barry went over the ones he'd received and guessed that Turd was building a shit army, since Obidon had said the demon would perform the same ritual used to summon it.

And how would Barry find the evil little shit?

Barry thought for a moment. If Turd was indeed building an army of shits, where would be the best place to do so? It would have to be moist, safe, out of the sunlight, and in a remote area, large enough to amass an army, a place no one would find, at least not without effort.

He thought long and hard. Maybe the school. There were showers there, a basement, locker room . . . No, school was still in session—there'd be too many people around.

He continued to think, trying to come up with some place, a remote place. The woods? Nope. Then it hit him—the industrial park. Barry and his friends—hell a lot of the neighborhood kids—went there for kicks, just to hang out, smoke cigarettes, break bottles and stuff. Almost everyone spray-painted the buildings. The older kids used it for parties. There were a number of warehouses and factories that had closed down, the places long-abandoned for years. Factories were spacious and vast, but he had no idea if they were moist. He supposed some were, especially if they had showers or some kind of steam room.

*   *   *

The next day, Barry woke early and rode his bike to the industrial park. Chambers Street was the main rode that led into the area. A few big rigs rumbled by, one even honking its horn after he signaled for the trucker to do so.

Barry bicycled along the worn asphalt, the hot May sun beating down upon him, oven-like. Turd would never survive long in this environment, which meant the little shit was going to be inside. Spotting the demon and his crew wouldn't be easy.

He checked around the first two abandoned factories, but both places were locked up tight. Whether or not Turd was inside, he didn't know. He proceeded to the next decrepit building.

The *For Sale* sign was still upright on the lawn, but was covered in graffiti. The building looked like all the others. It was kind of dilapidated in appearance, with broken windows and a gate that was chained closed. The place was set apart from the other buildings, next to a thick tree line, with acres of woods taking up the land behind it. Barry thought the structure would make for a great horror movie shoot, one where teens went, got lost, and were stalked by a disfigured mutant hungry for human flesh. Besides that, he also thought it would make for a great hideout.

Barry stashed his bike behind a copse of berry bushes and headed along the side of the building to the rear, where the loading bays where located. Along with his and his friends' graffiti tags were other people's names and drawings. There were a lot of penises, vaginas, and skulls. Barry didn't know why such things were so popular, but for some reason, kids liked drawing those three items the most.

He knew some of the older kids broke into the abandoned buildings to hang out and party, and he was counting on this for possible entry. The police had been cracking down, hence the reason the places he went to before this one were locked up tight.

All three loading bay doors were closed, and there was no way to open them—not that he was strong enough, anyway.

He tried a normal-sized door set between two of the bay doors, but it didn't budge.

Ready to move on, he noticed a pair of double doors at the end of the building, partially hidden behind a dented, green dumpster that contained a number of large rusted-out holes, allowing him to see beer cans and cigarette boxes inside. Someone had clearly positioned the receptacle there to keep the entrance hidden, but left enough room for the doors to be opened.

Barry made his way over to it, not getting his hopes up, when he noticed a brown trail leading across the bay landing. Upon closer inspection, he saw the trail was made up of, hundreds of tiny footprints.

Unable to step around the prints, he walked over them. They were dry and flaked away under his weight. He grabbed the door handle on the right, and pulled.

The door creaked open.

Barry cringed, immediately putting a hand to his face. The smell was awful, reminding him of when Suzy shat herself. He'd found Turd's lair, and the odor would only worsen the closer he came to the fecal army.

Barry backed away, inhaled a few lungfulls of air, then went in, closing the door behind him.

Normally, searching such a vast place would take hours, especially if it had a basement, but now all he had to do was follow the brown footprints.

Barry breathed through his mouth as he cautiously moved down a tan-colored hallway, the sheetrock walls nicked and dinged throughout. He passed by a number of offices, the rooms dusty and strewn with beer cans, coffee cups, cigarette butts, and condom wrappers.

Finally, the hallway ended, opening up to an

airplane hangar-sized room, filled with large gray tankers with the words, DANGER: FLAMMABLE GAS, printed on the sides. Machines the size of school buses took up most of the floor space around the tanks.

The shit tracks led straight through the center of the room. Barry followed them to a stairwell.

Taking each step as if a landmine might be present, Barry worked his way to the basement level and found himself standing in front of a closed door with a large, sandblasted window. Stenciled across the glass were the faded, but legible, words: *Men's Locker Room*. Written in black magic marker below this was: *No pussies allowed unless they're female*.

Barry giggled and breathed through his nose. He immediately regretted it, as the odor was much stronger, the air saturated with fecal particles. Feeling

161

the need to vomit, he quickly covered his nose and mouth with his shirt, closed his eyes, and counted to twenty, thinking of Suzy and how great she must've looked when she was in his shower naked—after she cleaned herself.

Suddenly, Barry stood tall, letting his shirt fall back into place, but remembering to breathe only through his mouth. Men's locker rooms had showers! And this place was huge. It would probably have multiple showers, like the locker room at the gym Barry's dad belonged to. There'd be plenty of room for an army to bathe in and remain moist.

Barry opened the door a crack and peered inside. His eye watered as powerful fumes struck it, minute fecal flakes coating his mouth and filling his lungs. Seeing no guards, he opened the door and slipped into the locker room.

A long bench extended between two rows of ceiling-high, gray-peeling lockers before the room took a right turn.

Barry took a step forward, seeing the shit-trail separate around the wooden bench where it came together again and disappeared around the corner. He heard a banging sound from one of the lockers on his right. The door flew open, and two rather large shit monsters sprung from within. They landed in front of him, each wearing an angry scowl and growling. They had long, nasty-looking clawed hands that looked more than capable of gutting a small dog in seconds.

Barry knew if he hesitated, they'd either attack him or run for help. So he lunged forward and brought his right foot down on the demon on his right, smashing the pliable fecal demon to death in an instant. Brown sludge shot out from underneath his foot like a stepped-on ketchup packet. Those things were scary, smelly, and could cut a person with their claws, which would lead to quite an infection if not properly treated, but they sure were weak in structure.

The other fecal demon screamed and took off running, disappearing around the corner of lockers.

Barry couldn't allow it to alert the others, and chased off after it. The little shit was fast. The main corridor of the locker room was benchless and wide enough for Barry to really pump his arms and run. Looking ahead, he saw a sign that read *Showers* with an arrow indicating to go left.

Barry dug deep within himself and pushed harder, then dove and stretched his arms and fingers, catching the demon on its right leg. The shit stumbled and fell face-first, but it was far from finished.

Grumbling, it pushed itself up.

Barry couldn't let it get away. He lunged forward on his hands and knees, bringing a fist down upon the shit-demon, smashing its lower half. The soft form gave easily, becoming nothing more than a large smear, but it was still alive.

With only an upper torso, the thing pulled itself forward, grunting with effort.

Panic and rage filled Barry's mind. He reached out, wrapped his hands around the fecal monster, and squeezed the life out of it, the soft, dark brown matter oozing between his fingers like cake batter.

A feeling of pride and victory soared through Barry, but it was short-lived when he realized how much work he still had to do.

Using his hands, he scooped up the demon's corpse and stashed it in one of the lockers, then scraped the shit off his hands as best as possible, leaving plenty of excrement around and under his nails.

Barry moved into the tiled hallway that led to the showers. The floor was covered with slick feces, and he took care to step cautiously.

When he reached the end of the hallway, he peered around the corner and into the shower room. The place was bathed in a goopy brown sludge. There had to be hundreds of the fecal demons within the substance, rolling around or simply wading in it. Each showerhead was set to trickle, keeping the area moist and allowing the army to remain solid.

Barry ducked back behind the wall, swallowing the lump in his throat. He'd found Turd's hideout, but at the same time he had no idea how he'd be able to stop so many.

Tip-toeing back out, he hurried through the locker room, cleaning up the first demon guard he killed, then left, finally catching his breath when he stood outside next to the dumpster.

Pulling out his cell phone, he called information and asked for the number to the Sparks' residence. The woman said there was a Fred H. Sparks on Cedar Street, and Barry told her that was it. He thanked the woman, hung up, then dialed the number.

"Hello?" asked a familiar sounding voice.

"Suzy?"

"Who's this?"

"It's Barry. I—"

"Barry," she said, heatedly. "You've got some nerve, but I guess it's cause you're slow or something, so let me make myself clear. I. Never. Want. To. Talk. To. You—"

"Just listen," Barry said, cutting off her words. "The demon isn't dead. In fact, it's raising an army. I need your help to stop them."

"What? No. No fucking way! Your demon. Your problem."

"But . . . hello?" Barry looked at his phone and saw that he had no connection. Suzy had hung up. He shook his head and dialed her number again.

"This better not be Barry Gilbert," she said. "It better be someone who just killed him and found his phone."

"Haven't you been watching the news?" Barry asked. "People are dead. I mean, you, yourself, were possessed by this thing. Don't you want to stop it?"

"Who's dead?"

"Mike, Brett, Devin . . . their whole families."

"Bullshit."

"Don't you watch the news?"

"Hell no. If it doesn't have hot guys and girls in it, I don't bother."

"Well go turn on the news. The story's all over, on every channel."

"Fine." She disconnected again.

Barry was tempted to call her back, but waited.

He'd give her some time. Let her see the awful news, it did involve her friends after all.

A few minutes later, his phone rang with a new number. He wasn't going to answer it, then remembered he'd called Suzy on her house phone. Maybe she was calling him back on her cell.

"Hello?" he said, putting the phone to his ear.

"Those were *my* friends," she said, coldly, as if they had been her possessions and not real people. "What the fuck did you do, Barry?"

"Now do you see why we have to stop Turd and his army of fecal terror?"

"This is all your fault," she cried. Barry could feel her anger like little fists beating against his skull. "You got my friends killed."

"I'm really sorry about that." Barry felt his heart sink, the entirety of the situation gripping him like a giant glove. Tears welled in his eyes. He blinked them away, needing to get a hold of himself. He needed to be action-hero-ready right now. There'd be time for crying later—when he was alone in his room or in the arms of his beloved Suzy.

"Hate me all you want," he said, hoping that wasn't the case, "but I need your help. No one else will ever believe me."

"Fine. But I want you to know that I think you're a real asshole. Now, what do we have to do?"

"Meet me in the industrial park. I'll be waiting in front of the third abandoned factory on the left. Oh, and bring a pair of high boots, fishing ones if you have them. It might get a bit messy."

*   *   *

Suzy hung up the phone. She stared at the news report, the volume on the TV muted. She couldn't believe her friends were dead. They had been members of her clique. She had been the ringleader, the one in charge. She'd cultivated those people thoroughly, hand-picking them over time, ensuring she had the *best* friends in the whole school.

At this very moment, she ground her teeth and clenched her fists. She wanted to kill Barry. It was assholes like him, the loners, losers, and freaks that wound up either making something of their lives or becoming psychos and hurting people, who went off the deep end because of ridicule and torment. Sure, her friends could be dickheads at times, but they were entitled to be because they were at the top of the high school food chain. They were good-looking, on the football team, had great grades, and were headed for big things. None of them would have ever summoned a demon. *How fucking pathetic!*

Suzy turned off the television. She needed to forget about Barry and what he had caused. For now, she needed to help the little loser kill his demon and its little turd army.

She went to the basement and found her dad's fishing gear. She grabbed his fly-fishing overalls—the things came up to her armpits. She wasn't sure what was going to happen but figured she'd take Barry's advice.

Next, she went out to the garage, grabbed her bicycle, and pedaled off to meet Barry.

Ten minutes later and a little sweaty, she met up with him. The kid was sitting on the curb. He looked sad, and she felt bad for him. He didn't have many friends and the ones he did have were losers like himself. She guessed the world needed them, for why else would they be in existence? Of course, Barry still deserved to be punished for his part in her friends' deaths, even though he hadn't done or condoned any of the killings.

She rode up to him, skidding out in fashionable style.

CHAPTER 15

Barry saw Suzy coming down the street. She was pedaling fast. Her face was rigid, serious, maybe even angry. *Good*, he thought. Better to have her serious and focused than a wreck and crying. Yes, having her mad was much better for them both. There'd be time for crying later.

Suzy kept coming in fast, and for a moment, Barry caught her stare and could've sworn she meant to run him over, but at the last moment she skidded out, the rear tire of her bike stopping an inch from his foot.

"Where are they?" she asked, her chest heaving.

"Stash your bike behind those bushes alongside mine and follow me."

After hiding her bike, she and Barry headed toward the rear of the building. Barry told her everything that happened since he had arrived, including how he took out two demon turds.

"Gross," Suzy said, flinching away from him. "You squeezed it with your bare hand?" She shivered. "Keep those mitts of yours away from me."

Normally, having had shit smeared on his hand would've made Barry want to wash his skin clean with soap and hot water, even squirt a blob of hand sanitizer to make sure the germs were definitely killed, like whenever he wiped his ass and the toilet paper ripped, which happened once in awhile. But now, he just didn't give a damn, and had even picked his nose, removing a ticklish booger that had been bothering him while he waited for Suzy.

They reached the open door at the back of the building. Barry went over the plan.

"That's it?" Suzy asked. "You're going to stomp them to death?"

"It's the surest bet, I think. Their bodies are weak, easily destructible."

Suzy thought for a moment and nodded. "I agree. The only other way would be to dry the things out, but given their current location that wouldn't work too well."

"It's pretty awful-smelling down there, so breathe through your mouth or you'll hurl."

Suzy opened her mouth and practiced. "Okay, I'm good."

They followed the fecal trail through the machine

room and down the stairwell to the locker room door. Suzy cringed and pinched her nose. Her eyes watered up, and Barry thought she was going to lose it.

"You breathed through your nose, didn't you?" he whispered.

Suzy's eyes were closed, her face scrunched up. She held up a finger, then nodded and opened her eyes a few moments later. "You're an idiot, Barry."

"Me? I warned you not to—"

"No, why didn't you tell me to bring nose plugs? Or Vick's VapoRub to smear under the nose. My dad's a surgeon; he's got all sorts of useful stuff."

"Sorry about that. I guess I wasn't thinking." He looked at her worriedly.

"What is it?"

"You can't mess up like that again. The smell is ten times worse behind this door."

Suzy's eyes narrowed. She slowly shook her head, clearly pissed off.

"How was I supposed to know it would smell so bad?" he asked.

She swatted him on the arm. "It's your turd demon, you should know." She rolled her eyes in disbelief.

Barry thought about asking her why *she* hadn't thought to bring nose plugs if she was so brilliant, but didn't want the added confrontation. He needed her focused on the shits, not him.

"Just breathe through your mouth," he said.

"The quicker we get this over with, the faster we can get the hell out of here."

"And keep an eye out for guards."

Barry crept up to the locker room and pushed it open. He peered inside and saw that the area was clear and waved for Suzy to follow. They moved in, letting the door shut softly behind them. Barry crept up to where the first row of lockers ended and peered around the corner where the second demon had attempted to flee. Straight ahead, about thirty feet away, was the entrance to the showers.

"I think I'm going to be sick," Suzy whispered in his ear, nearly causing Barry to get a stiffy.

Barry turned around. Suzy's face had lost all its color.

"The air," she said. "I have to keep swallowing, and I can feel the shit particles sticking to the roof of my mouth and tongue, entering my lungs. It's like breathing in diesel soot, except I know it's shit soot."

Barry saw her shaking. He needed to calm her down. "I know it's bad—"

Suzy spun around and ran to the locker room door. She reached out to grab the handle, but instead bent over and vomited. Pink-hued sludge, chunky, like strawberry oatmeal, splattered onto the floor, door, and her feet, the booted overalls shielding her.

Barry thought the gig was up when he saw her bent over with vomit coming out. Everything seemed to be happening in slow motion. Their presence would be known. But Suzy puked quietly, hardly making a sound. The impact of her vomit was the loudest part, like dumping a bucket of runny mud.

Suzy remained bent over, one hand on the back of the door. Puke-laced saliva dripped from her lips. She was holding her nose again with her free hand and taking deep breaths. Her body jerked and she puked again, adding to the pile of vomit on the floor and further dirtying her father's fishing overalls. She stood there for a few moments, wiped her mouth on her sleeve, then stood and looked at Barry. She gave him the thumbs-up sign.

Barry hurried over to her, making sure to keep his nose pinched. He tried to avoid looking at her stomach's contents, but couldn't help it. It was nasty.

He'd now witnessed the girl of his dreams shit herself and vomit. But looking at her, even with a small chunk of upchuck in her golden hair, he still wanted her.

He'd press his lips against hers in a second if she'd let him, rinsed mouth or not.

"Why are you staring at me like that?" she asked.

"Um . . . just wanted to make sure you're okay." He reached out and plucked the thrown-up chunk of undigested food from her hair and tossed it away.

"Thanks," she said, "I'm usually so careful when I puke. I'm actually quite professional at it, you know from all those parties I go to. Can't afford to pack on the pounds. I save my calories for healthy stuff." She took a breath and smiled. "I feel better now. Just have to remember to breathe through my mouth."

They made their way back to where the lockers ended. Barry checked around the corner again before the two companions made their way to the shower room entrance.

"Okay," Barry said. "You stay here and make sure no turds escape. Stomp any you see. I'm going in." He looked at her. "You good?"

She nodded and swallowed.

Barry did a few quick deep-knee bends. He had a lot of stomping to do and didn't want to cramp up. Finished, he felt shaky, his heart beating fast, and headed down the tile corridor. He stopped just before the shower room, took quick breaths to pump himself up and stepped out from behind the wall.

The room looked the same as before, shits everywhere, bathing in brown murky water. He spotted Turd instantly, the demon's size and red glowing eyes differentiating it from the others, whose eyes glowed yellow. Turd was sitting halfway up on the wall in a soap dish.

None of the demons had spotted Barry yet, which surprised him. He took advantage and headed in, stomping away at the shits below his feet. He smashed two with ease, then three and four.

Turd pointed a clawed finger at him, shouting something in demon-tongue. The demon king's eyes were a fierce red, his face a scowl of anger.

Barry ignored Turd and continued to stomp the creatures to death. Demons ran at him, their tiny claws bared, mouths wide, teeth showing like sharpened pieces of rice. Shit crumpled and splattered beneath Barry's feet, sludgy water splashing over the room. His shoes were clotted with feces and soaked through to his socks. He'd never wear either of the items again.

Barry made it to the center of the room, continuing to crush his foes. The ones that flew at him were battered away or smushed against his body, caking him in shit. He was doing the poopy dance of poopy dances, the one to end them all. But he was growing tired, the shit becoming like mud, making his movements sluggish. The shit floor was closing in on him and he began to worry. He felt a nick here and there as demons made it past his swinging arm defense. They sliced his flesh with their talons. Barry couldn't stomp fast enough, his breath coming faster as his body demanded more air. Turd was still on his perch, growling in demon.

More and more demons were launching themselves at him, coming from all directions. More claws dug into him, tearing at his clothes and flesh. He spun around, no longer stomping, trying to get the things off of him. He swatted at himself. Demons landed on his face; he bit them in half, tasting the putrescence, vomiting, continuing to fight and splat the shits. They smeared themselves over his eyes, clogged his nostrils, and were trying to enter his mouth.

Blinded and unable to breathe, Barry felt himself fading. He needed to open his mouth for a gulp of air, but as soon as he did, a shit demon would find its way inside.   This was it, bested by shit.

About to give in, he felt something swipe at his right cheek. Fingers scraped over his mouth, the shits no longer there, trying to get in. Still unable to see, he opened his mouth and took in a gulp of fetid air. It was the best fetid air he'd ever had.

Wiping at his eyes, he saw Suzy. She was swatting away at the demon shits on his body. He heard Turd howl, the demon's voice all too familiar. Looking around the room, he saw that the showerheads were on full blast, steam rising from the floor, the water set to hot. Suzy was brilliant.

Feeling recharged, Barry joined Suzy in stomping, sending pieces of feces everywhere. He wondered why he hadn't thought to use the showers as a weapon. The force, heat, and water made it difficult for the demons to stay solid, stay alive.

Steam filled the shower room. Barry grew hot as he continued to kill, the mud-like shit now looser and easy to move through.

"Suzy, you're a genius," he shouted.

"You can compliment me later," she said, "after we finish off all these smelly little bastards."

The two companions continued to stomp and swat away the demons. The steam was making the shits' bodies nothing more than goo. Claws fell from their hands and feet, and eyes drooped, appearing less menacing. Some tried to flee, but their movements were pathetic and slow.

Barry and Suzy were making easy work of them.

Barry glanced across the room through the rolling clouds of steam and saw Turd, the demon's malevolent red eyes staring at him like a beacon in the night. The little demon picked up the bar of soap it was standing on and launched it across the room. Barry thought the little guy's aim was off until he saw where it was going—toward Suzy, who was finishing off the last of Turd's army.

Barry yelled for her to watch out. She turned just as the soap collided with her forehead. He heard a dull clunk. Suzy's eyes went wide. Her legs buckled and she crashed to the sludge-covered floor. Barry shielded himself with his arms as the brown muck splashed over him.

He ran to her, wanting to make sure she was okay, realizing his mistake when he reached her. Pain exploded in his back as Turd landed on him, the demon sinking its claws into his flesh. Turd ran up Barry's spine to his head, using its nails to keep from slipping off. Barry reached around to grab the demon shit, but yelped in pain when the little shit closed its jaw around his finger, biting him. He pulled his hand back and whipped it in the air, now worried to death that he'd suffer from E. Coli poisoning if he didn't get it cleaned soon.

Movement on his right caught his attention. He turned and saw Suzy getting to her feet, though looking a little dazed and weak in the knees. Turd clawed at Barry's head, ripping out hair and flesh. Barry brought up a hand to swat the demon, but it was too agile and had sprung upward, slicing a deep gash into Barry scalp as he went.

Barry howled in pain. He needed to do something before the demon did some real damage. As it was he might be on his way to bleeding to death or getting E. Coli poisoning. Barry's scalp felt like it was on fire as the demon continued to slice. Barry used both hands to whack the demon, hoping to catch it off guard, but every time he attempted an attack, Turd clawed his hands. His head felt like it was burning up. Then he thought, *Fire! That's it!*

Barry reached up and grabbed onto Turd, despite the pain of getting cut up, then hurried over to one of the showerheads and stood under the stream. The hot water was scalding, but would be worth the pain if it did its job.

He felt Turd's body melt away, the demon's howls turning to garbled cries, his solid form becoming mush. A river of brown flowed down Barry's body and across the floor. He backed out of the stream and looked at his hands. They practically glowed red from the hot water. Underneath his nails were the last remnants of Turd. He shoved his hands back under the stream and cleaned them as thoroughly as possible.

When all the brown was out from under his nails, he turned around and saw Suzy. "Are they all dead?" she asked, rubbing a lump on her forehead, her clothes dripping wet.

"Yeah. They're all gone, including Turd. Killed him myself."

"Good, cause if I don't get out of here now, no amount of therapy will help me."

They stripped down to their undergarments and showered off after adjusting the water temperature. They rinsed their clothing, too. Barry promised not to look at her while she cleaned herself, but managed a few glances now and then, and was glad he did. Even amongst the horrendous odor, shit, bleeding wounds, and everything that had happened, he couldn't stop thinking how beautiful she was, and hoped that today's events would bring them closer, maybe give him a chance. Hell, he'd do her right where she was, shit-covered or not.

When they were finished, clothes stained but wearable, they left the locker room, dripping wet.

Outside, Suzy dried out under the hot sun by lying

on the cement loading bay. Barry waited for her in the shade. His skin was practically glowing red from the hot water burns on his hands and head.

"We have a bond for life now," he said, bored while she was drying off.

"Not one I want to remember."

"So, any chance you'd want to get together this week?"

Suzy laughed, but it wasn't a jolly one. "You're lucky I don't kill you."

Barry had thought the answer would be no, but took a gamble. Oh well, at least he had a chance to see her almost naked.

Suzy sat up. "Clothes are pretty much dry. I'm out

of here."

"See you in school, then?"

She hopped down from the bay's ledge and walked over to Barry. "I want nothing to do with you. You ruined my clique. Almost got me killed and caused me to battle shit monsters. I need to pretend this didn't happen, that it was all a dream. Don't you dare utter a word to me, again—ever! If you so much as look at me, I'll cut off your balls and make you eat them." With that, she walked away, leaving a stunned Barry standing alone.

The next day, Barry saw Suzy at school, standing at her locker. Her usual crowd was nowhere to be seen because most of them dead. He went up to her and said, "Hi." She stared at him, her face unreadable. She shook her head. "So sad. So very sad." She turned and walked away.

*   *   *

Two days later, Barry was sitting in his room when his phone rang. He looked at the Caller I.D. and saw that it was Suzy. His pulse quickened. He couldn't believe it. Maybe the girl had a change of heart. He picked up the phone. It turned out she was sorry. It was all the stress that had messed up her head. She liked him, and wanted to hang out. "Can't blame a girl after she lost her friends, can you?"

"No, definitely not," he said.

They met at Larry's Diner in town, had a couple of

burgers with fries, then went for a walk in the woods.

"I want to show you something," she said, veering off the main trail—one Barry knew quite well—and heading down a smaller one. It ended in a small clearing. There was an old wooden table with a white tablecloth on it. Next to the table was a tray, with what appeared to be surgical equipment on it.

"What the heck is this?" he asked, then felt a small prick on the side of his neck. A moment later, the world went dark.

Barry awoke sometime later, tied to a chair. Birds chirped in the distance. He was groggy and couldn't move his legs. In fact, he couldn't *feel* his legs. A small dinner tray table with a bowl of steaming soup on it had been placed in front of him.

"Hungry?" a female voice asked. Suzy walked out

from behind him. She was wearing a blood-spattered white apron and smiling. In her left hand was a scalpel, the blade had red on it.

"What's going on?" he asked, nervously. "Why am I tied up? And why can't I move my legs?"

"The not-being-able-to-move part is thanks to an epidural I gave you. By the way, your back might be a little sore once it wears off. I'm going to be a surgeon one day like my dad. Practice makes perfect."

"I don't understand . . ."

"I know you're probably a little groggy from the drugs I gave you, but here it is: I warned you to stay away from me, not to talk to me." She stepped up to him, holding the tip of the scalpel under his right eye. "You made me so mad, so I had to act, and maybe lost a little control, but ultimately I think I did a bang up job. Now eat your ball soup. Hotdog's next."

Barry looked down and saw bandages around his crotch, the white cloth soaked with red. He looked at Suzy, and screamed.

The End

David Bernstein

BIZARRO PULP PRESS

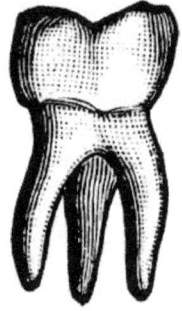

WWW.BIZARROPULPPRESS.COM

FECAL TERROR